Issac Taylor

**Leaves From an Egyptian Note-Book**

Issac Taylor

**Leaves From an Egyptian Note-Book**

ISBN/EAN: 9783337227272

Printed in Europe, USA, Canada, Australia, Japan

Cover: Foto ©Andreas Hilbeck / pixelio.de

More available books at **www.hansebooks.com**

# LEAVES

# EGYPTIAN NOTE-BOOK

# LEAVES

FROM AN

# EGYPTIAN NOTE-BOOK

BY

## ISAAC TAYLOR

M.A., LITT. D., HON. LL.D.

CANON OF YORK

LONDON

KEGAN PAUL, TRENCH & CO., 1, PATERNOSTER SQUARE

1888

# PREFACE.

—◦—

NARRATIVES of Egyptian travel being already sufficiently abundant, I have not attempted to add another to the list. The scope of this volume is wholly different. It consists, for the most part, of notes of conversations with Egyptians on politics and religion.

I went to Egypt, the head-quarters of Islam, in order to investigate the truth of certain assertions which have of late been freely made as to the barbarism, ignorance, profligacy, and intolerance of Mahommedan nations. My inquiries were facilitated by the fact that some of my pleas for a better mutual understanding between Christians and Mahommedans had been recently reproduced, with appreciative comments, in the vernacular journals of Cairo, Beyrout, and Constantinople·

Hence I found, somewhat to my surprise, that my name and my opinions were not unknown to Mahommedan gentlemen, who placed at my disposal means of information not accessible to ordinary tourists. I have held long and interesting discussions, not only with Europeans resident in Egypt, and with men who fill important posts in the Egyptian government, but with Moslems of every class, who have conversed, without reserve, on the tenets of Islam, and on the condition and prospects of their country and their religion. I have also been allowed to visit many of the schools and colleges of Cairo, and have talked freely with the students and teachers, and have examined several of the classes.

What has been told me may not always have been the truth, but at all events it has been that which my informants wished me to believe; and it is not unimportant to know what Moslems desire that Christians should think as to the tenets and practices of their religion. I have, as far as possible, checked the information given me by personal observation. The conclusions at which I have arrived differ so widely from the views prevalent in England, that I believe I shall be doing a real service to the cause of truth and charity by placing them on record. And if I seem to have stated my opinions somewhat dogmatically, I have done so simply for the sake of brevity. Neither have I considered it necessary perpetually to reaffirm my belief in the immeasurable superiority of our own religion and civilization to those of Egypt, these being matters on which my readers have doubtless formed their own conclusions.

I find that comparatively few travellers seek or obtain opportunities of conversing confidentially with Mahommedans on the subject of their beliefs as to which they are usually reticent, in accordance with a precept of the Koran, which forbids them to argue with Christians in the spirit of hostile controversy. But since, in India and elsewhere, we have at least fifty millions of Mahommedan fellow-subjects, it cannot be unimportant for us to know how far they agree or differ from us in their way of looking at fundamental questions of science, morals, politics, and religion. Considering also the peculiar relations in which we stand to Egypt, it seems desirable that we should not be ignorant of what the Egyptians think of our occupation of their country, of our methods of administration, and of the reforms we have introduced.

The greater portion of these notes originally appeared in the *St. James's Gazette*, and I have to thank the proprietors of that journal for permission to reprint them. Two descriptive papers—the first and the last—have been added, and the rest have been revised, and, in some instances, considerably enlarged.

I. T.

SETTRINGTON RECTORY, YORK,
*June*, 1888.

# CONTENTS.

# LEAVES

FROM AN

# EGYPTIAN NOTE-BOOK.

—◦◦◦—

## I.

### STREET-LIFE IN CAIRO.

On visiting a strange city of which we have heard
much, the first impression is usually one of dis-
appointment. This is notably the case with Rome,
where superficial meanness and squalor disguise
unequalled interest and real magnificence. Venice
is an exception to the rule, and so, perhaps,
are Nürnberg and Prag. But Cairo is so utterly
different from anything in Europe—the outdoor
life is so amusing, the streets, with their moving
diorama of brilliant colour and marvellous costume,
so picturesque—that the most exacting traveller
can hardly be disappointed, however highly he
may have pitched his expectations.

B

In the new quarter, which strives to imitate a
European city, the streets are broad boulevards,
shaded by dense avenues of the dark, evergreen
*lebbek*, a kind of acacia; the house-fronts are
splendid with crimson Bougainvilleas, and other
creepers, their forecourts and gardens overgrown
with thickets of palms, orange-trees, bamboos,
or bananas, giving a semi-tropical aspect to the
thoroughfares.   Here we meet the carriages of
English officials or of wealthy pashas, each pre-
ceded by a running footman or *sais*, barefooted and
barelegged, clad in a gorgeous costume of snowy
muslin and scarlet cloth or silk, embroidered with
gold thread, a blue tassel hanging from the head-
dress, and bearing in his hand a long light wand
to clear a free passage through the streets.

From the new quarter—a sort of sub-tropical
Paris, with clubs and hotels where the society is as
English as at Meurice's or at Brighton—we plunge
in a few minutes into the heart of the old city,
with bazaars and mosques as oriental as those
of Damascus, and where, at every turn, we are
reminded of the strange fairyland of the "Arabian
Nights."   We meet ungainly camels strutting
through the streets; water-carriers bending under
the weight of huge water-skins; veiled women with
their infants, not in arms as with us, but seated

astride on the mother's shoulder; ladies in black, with their gauzy, balloon-like drapery floating behind them, going to pay visits, mounted upon donkeys; turbaned Turks; black-robed mollahs; stately Arab sheikhs, and Africans of every hue, from the clear, transparent yellow-brown of Egypt to the shining jet of Nubia. Here, in the older quarters of the town, shade trees are not needed; the unpaved streets, with their projecting oriels of latticed woodwork, are so narrow as nearly to exclude the midday sun, while the bazaars, still narrower, are spanned from house to house by a loose roof of interlaced palm leaves and bamboos, softening the glare, while admitting from the cloudless sky such light as may be needful.

Each bazaar is appropriated to a different trade or nationality. The Turkish bazaar, the Tunis bazaar, the Syrian bazaar, the carpet bazaar, and the bazaars of the slipper-makers, the brass-workers, the silversmiths, and the fez-makers are, perhaps, the most picturesque. They are mostly too narrow to permit the passage of a carriage, while a camel loaded with a huge bundle of sugar-canes will completely block the thoroughfare. The traveller threads his way through the dense crowd on foot, or, more usually, on a donkey, the attendant shouting the needful directions to his employer or to the passers by. "*Ya sitt, shemah'lik,*" "Oh, lady! to thy left!" "*U'wa, ya Uchte,*" "Take care, oh, my sister!" "*Yamenik, ya howaghah,*" "To thy right, oh, traveller!" The noise is deafening, but the busy scene is most amusing.

As you thus pass through a bazaar, mounted on a donkey—which, if the traveller is an Englishman, is probably called Mrs. Langtry, or Gran' Ole Man; if he is an American, Jumbo or Yankee Doodle; if a German, Rameses or Bismarck—you look down from your convenient elevation on the artisans plying their trades, or the shopkeepers leisurely sipping coffee or smoking their hookahs, as they squat cross-legged on the raised divan which forms the entrance to the windowless and doorless recess which constitutes the shop. The whole stock-in-trade is usually displayed upon the walls, or laid out upon the floor. If you dismount to bargain for some attractive bit of Oriental workmanship, coffee and cigarettes are produced as a preliminary to any serious transaction, which sometimes requires repeated visits to effect. On the first occasion you inspect the goods, depreciate their excellence, and ask the price. The owner politely declines to name it; he leaves it entirely to you, and desires to know what your Excellency may be disposed to give. You offer half of what

you suppose to be the value, and the owner
suggests a sum treble that which he intends ultimately to accept.  You state that you are poor ;
he rejoins it is well known that all Englishmen
are fabulously rich.  You part with apparent
rancour, and the next time you pass you look
regretfully at the article ; the merchant accosts you
as a dear friend, and solely, as he affirms, with
the object of securing the goodwill of one so much
esteemed, proposes to sell you the goods at about
twice their value.  Friends of the shopkeeper, who
represent themselves as disinterested spectators,
crowd round and extol the beauty of the goods,
or are astonished at the ridiculous insignificance
of the price demanded.  Finally, after a consulta-
tion with your dragoman, you name your " last
word," and the merchant exclaims effusively,
" Take it, it is yours," with the air of generously
bestowing on you a valuable gift.  The little
comedy is over, and the actors and spectators
separate with mutual expressions of satisfaction
and esteem.

In all this there is, I think, no dishonesty or
intention to deceive ; it is simply the custom of
the country, and the shopkeeper would feel
defrauded of his rights if he were deprived of the
amusement of bargaining.  I heard of a gentleman,

unused to Eastern ways, at once giving for a splendid brass tray the price first asked—a napoleon. His companion said he would take the fellow to it, and offered a napoleon. "No," said the shop-keeper; "your friend gave me what I asked, and I expected he would beat me down; but as he did not, you shall have the other for ten francs."

Most noticeable is the extreme good-nature, dignity, and natural politeness of all you meet. Foot-passengers make way for each other with obliging good-humour and mutual compliments, street rows or quarrels are rare, a drunken man is never seen, the police are conspicuous by their absence, and you look in vain for any exhibition of the surliness, ruffianism, and brutality of Western cities. Moslems are enjoined by their religion to be merciful to animals, and in this respect Cairo contrasts most favourably with Naples. Passers-by are always ready to help the stranger out of a difficulty, or to supply any aid or information that may be required. The considerateness of people of the labouring class shows itself at every turn. On one occasion, the saddle-girth of a young lady of our party gave way, and she had to dismount in the midst of a noisy wedding procession, in one of the lowest quarters of the town. She had some difficulty in remounting, as her donkey was frightened by the noise of the tom-toms, and the stirrup could not be refixed. The donkey-man evidently feeling some delicacy in lifting a lady in the presence of the crowd, a gigantic negress stepped forward of her own accord, and with native grace took her up in her arms and placed her in the saddle. An incident which would probably have excited the rude derision of a low-class English crowd, was in Egypt the occasion of ready and considerate helpfulness.

European ladies are treated by the natives with respectful deference, no impertinent or insulting remarks being offered in their hearing. The donkey-men seem to regard them as angelic beings, who, by some mysterious custom, are allowed the strange liberty, denied to women of their own race, of going about unveiled. The easy courtesy and friendliness of manner which most ladies adopt towards their native guides confirm them in this impression, and I have never heard of an unseemly word or gesture having been addressed to ladies, who in the crowded streets sometimes become separated from their friends, and have to find their way back to their hotels with only the escort of a native attendant. A young girl, protected in her innocence only by the native chivalry of a Moslem donkey-boy, picked up casually in the street, would be far more safe from insult or injury in Cairo than, under similar chance escort, in the streets of Paris or of London.

No one can affirm that Cairo is a godless or irreligious city. Religion seems to exert a greater binding moral force on the conduct of the labouring classes than in London, Paris, or Berlin. It restrains men from evil, and tends to make them kindly, virtuous, and moral. Moslems certainly do endeavour to practise in their daily lives the precepts of gentleness, benevolence, and forgiveness of injuries which are so constantly inculcated in the Koran, and which are usually committed to memory at school. The Koran, for instance, asserts, "Whoso forgiveth and maketh peace shall find his reward for it from God." "Paradise is prepared for those who bridle their anger, and forgive men." "The servants of the Merciful are they who walk upon the earth softly, and when the ignorant speak unto them they reply, 'Peace!'" "Those who unjustly wrong others, and act insolently upon earth, verily, a grievous punishment awaiteth them." That these precepts constitute real motives for self-restraint there can be no doubt. Of course an occasional dispute arises in the crowded streets. Flowing robes of blue or yellow are for a moment mixed in seem-

ingly inextricable confusion; there is a half-friendly
tussle; but no blows are struck, as would be the
case in England, and in a few moments the dis-
putants, having recited some verse from the Koran
enjoining peace, are walking together reconciled—
if boys, with their arms round one another's necks,
or if negroes, showing their white teeth from ear
to ear in a grin of merriment.

The people are more given to outward religious
observances than in any other city I have ever
visited. "I like the Mussulman," said that stern
Puritan, General Gordon; "he is not ashamed of
his God, and his life is fairly pure." The mosques
are far better frequented by the labouring class
than churches are with us, although the mosque
is rather a convenience than a necessity of worship.
At the appointed hours men desist from their work,
and, turning their faces towards Mecca, openly
repeat their prayers in public places. The labourer
in the fields leaves his oxen or his camels, the
steersman on your Nile boat asks a friend to take
the helm, while, for a few moments, he prostrates
himself before the Lord of all the worlds, the
Merciful and the Compassionate, and beseeches
His guidance in the right way. At the Boulak
Museum, as the hour of devotion approaches, the
attendants one by one retire to the courtyard, and

there, surrounded by the statues of the gods of ancient Egypt, reverently repeat the appointed prayers.  What would be thought of such a scene at the British Museum or the Louvre?  It shows the essential difference between Eastern and Western notions of devotion and of propriety.

And what a strange thrill is felt by the stranger from the West when, at sunrise, he first hears the blind muezzin, with his musical intonation, calling from the summit of a neighbouring minaret to all good people to come to prayer, in the very words that have come down from the lifetime of the Prophet : " Allahu Akbar !  God is great ! . . . Come to prayer ! . . . Prayer is better than sleep ! . . . There is no god but Allah ! . . . He giveth life, and He dieth not ! . . . O Thou bountiful, Thy mercy ceaseth not ! . . . My sins are great, greater is Thy mercy ! . . . I extol His perfections ! . . . Allahu Akbar! God is great !"  And then, as these words are heard, all faithful people, after purifying themselves by the enjoined ablutions of face and feet and hands, reverently obey the call, first kneeling on the ground, and then touching the earth twice with their foreheads in humble adoration, as they confess that " God is great ;' there is none other than He !" and, when the prayers are finished, standing erect, with outstretched arms and extended palms, as if to receive the promised blessing descending from on high. The simple faith, reverence, and devoutness with which this is done, the worshipper wholly wrapt in his devotions, and utterly unconscious of the presence of by-standers, is inexpressibly touching. And the result of these constant devotions is, I think, undoubtedly manifested in the daily lives of these simple children of the Prophet.

The amount of crime in Cairo is extremely small. A Pasha of English birth, who is employed in the police administration, assured me that it is much less, in proportion to the population, than in London, Paris, or Berlin. The streets are safer and far more decent than those of London, and an unprotected woman can walk through them without fear of molestation. The police are relatively fewer than in any great European city, and are seldom seen. Robbery with violence is very rare, while the abstinence from alcohol so rigorously enjoined by the Mahommedan religion results in the absence of rowdyism. Drunken brawls occur, but the offenders belong mainly to the large foreign population, Maltese, Levantines, and Italians. The crimes of embezzlement and forgery are rarely committed except by Greeks and Coptic Christians. The patience, good-humour, gentleness, and dignity of the poorer classes, especially in the Mahommedan quarters, cannot fail to strike the most superficial observer.

There does not seem to be much extreme poverty or any absolute destitution, though there is nothing that corresponds to our poor law. The people seem sufficiently fed and clad ; the climate making boots, fuel, and meat needless luxuries. I am informed that deaths from starvation are unknown. To support the destitute is considered a meritorious act of religion ; the aged and infirm are clothed and fed by their relations, or, failing such, by compassionate neighbours. A sort of almshouse is supported by the Khedive ; but it is little needed, and the inmates are but few.

## II

## EDUCATION AND CULTURE.

IT is commonly supposed in England that Mahommedans are a species of barbarians, uncivilized, ignorant, bigoted, and fanatical. Canon Malcolm MacColl, for instance, has boldly asserted, in the columns of the *Times*, that "for every Moslem progress beyond the Koran is not only superfluous, but impious in addition." Such a statement is a ludicrous misconception of the facts. I confess that I was surprised to find how high a standard of intelligence and education prevails in the upper ranks of Mahommedan gentlemen. There are not a few who have been educated in Paris, or who have resided for a time in England, with whom it is possible to discuss politics and religion on terms of full equality. I do not say this class is very numerous ; but it exists, and with greater facilities for the higher education it might be increased very largely. One of the first visits I paid in Cairo was to a Mahommedan gentleman of Circassian blood, whose father had been a Mameluke. He is a sincere Moslem, firmly convinced of the superiority of Islam to Christianity. But this was no ignorant or fanatical belief. I found he had gone deeply into the question, and was an intelligent student of comparative religion. As I entered he laid down the book he was reading. It was Barthélemy Saint-Hilaire's work on "Boudha et sa Religion," and on the table beside him lay Renan's "Vie de Jésus." Glancing over the well-filled shelves of an extensive library, I found commentaries on the Koran, the Bible, and the Avesta; while the works of the Arabian mathematicians and philosophers stood side by side upon his shelves with those of Darwin and Herbert Spencer, together with Todhunter's "Differential Calculus" and sundry Cambridge text-books treating of the higher mathematics. On visiting another Pasha, a Mahommedan of Turkish extraction, the first question he asked me, as he read my card, was whether I was any relation to the discoverer of Taylor's Theorem, a fairly stiff piece of book-work in the Differential Calculus; and starting from this question the conversation turned for some time on the subject of the higher mathematics. I found him well acquainted with the relative merits and defects of the French and

English methods, and he said that he knew of no higher intellectual pleasure than the solution of problems in the Calculus. These were the first two Moslem gentlemen I visited in Cairo. How many morning calls would one have to pay in London before coming across hosts so intelligent and accomplished?

That such acquirements are not altogether exceptional I had proof the next day, when I visited one of the higher schools in Cairo, and was asked by the Pasha who accompanied me to examine the pupils in mathematics. Picking out one of the youths, and remembering my conversation of the previous day, I asked him to write out Taylor's Theorem on the black-board— a task which he performed correctly, explaining, as he went on, the difference between the English and Arabic notations. I then wrote on the slate the equations to certain curves of the third and fourth dimensions, and asked another lad to resolve and trace them—which was satisfactorily accomplished. Turning into one of the junior class-rooms, I selected for examination a lad ten years old, and was astonished at the rapidity and accuracy with which he demonstrated on the slate easy problems in plane geometry. In a similar secondary school in England, it would have been difficult indeed to find a boy of the same age who would have acquitted himself so well. And many of these boys, be it remembered, were able to converse with fair fluency in English and French as well as in Arabic.

These were secular schools, under the Minister for Education; and I was anxious to know whether the theological students at El Azhar, where instruction in the Koran forms the chief subject of study, considered " progress beyond the Koran " to be impious as well as superfluous. I found that the Sheikh el Azhar, the official who corresponds in his functions to the vice-chancellor of an English university, was desirous to obtain from the Minister of Education facilities for the instruction of 1200 of his students in the rudiments of secular science ; and I was taken to see an experimental class in which such instruction was being given. Here, if anywhere, one would expect to see Mahommedan narrowness, intolerance, and fanaticism ; but I found the students, all destined to be mollahs in Mahommedan mosques, intelligent and eager for information. They were then being instructed in geography. Some questions I asked as to the extent of the empire of the Mahommedan Khalifs in Spain were correctly answered. Tours was not marked on the map; but the site of

Charles Martel's victory was pointed out, and the students took eager interest in a brief account I gave them of the place occupied by the Mahommedan University of Cordova as the centre of scientific culture at a time when the rest of Europe was only emerging from barbarism. Seeing their quick intelligence, it seemed plain to me that El Azhar, which is resorted to by students from the whole of the vast region which lies between Morocco and Bokhara, might be made the source of culture and civilization for the whole Moslem world. The difficulty lies, not as has been asserted, in Mahommedan fanaticism and intolerance, but in the want of funds. The revenues of El Azhar are estimated to amount to between £15,000 and £20,000 a year ; but they can only be devoted to the subsistence of the students and to the provision of theological teaching. Anything more must be provided from without. The Egyptian Government is poor ; a pittance of £70,000 a year is all that can be spared for the Budget of Education. But if money could be found to provide a proper teaching staff in secular subjects, the great institution of El Azhar offers a unique opportunity for bringing Islam into line with Western science. What is most required at present is a sufficient education for the officials needed

C

to conduct the government of Egypt, for clerks in the Government offices, for engineers connected with the Department of Public Works, and above all for medical students. The School of Medicine has made great progress in recent years, but much still remains to be done.

The Egyptian is not wanting in quickness of apprehension or in aptitude for instruction. In these respects, more especially as regards mathematics and the acquirement of languages, his natural faculties surpass those of average English boys; what is wanting is fibre and moral tone. If Egypt is in future to be governed mainly by Egyptians, the higher posts in the service will have to be filled by natives who have been educated in Europe. The results of centuries of subserviency cannot be eradicated in a day. Trickery, falsehood, and bribery are not regarded with abhorrence; and young men brought up in Egypt do not comprehend the standard of personal honour which prevails among English gentlemen. At present the sons of wealthy families are usually sent to Paris to finish their education. Here they often become Anglophobists, or they imbibe revolutionary sentiments; in most cases they learn to drink and to gamble and to dance—accomplishments forbidden by their religion, and of no service to them whatever. It seems to me that the best prospect for Egypt would be for her future governors to be trained in England rather than in France. Surely it would not be impossible for one of the smaller Cambridge colleges to throw open its doors to the sons of Egyptian gentlemen, providing due security for the exercise of their religion, and taking care that their faith should not be tampered with by over-eager proselytizers.

I have been greatly struck by the absence of that intolerance which has been so freely imputed to Mahommedans. They are sincere believers, convinced of the truth of their religion and of its superiority to Christianity, and regarding apostasy from the faith of Islam as a grievous crime. On the other hand, there seems to be no desire to proselytize, and there is perfect tolerance and full religious liberty. Conversions from Christianity to Islam occasionally occur, but I am told that they are not desired or encouraged, converts seldom being very reputable persons. Christianity, however, entails no social disadvantages, and is no bar to office. Nubar Pasha, the most influential subject of the Khedive, is an Armenian Christian, and other Christian Pashas and Beys hold high office, while the lower clerkships are largely filled by Copts. Christians in

Cairo are regarded with a more intelligent tolerance than Mahommedans are in London, and I think it might even be affirmed that there is less religious fanaticism in Egypt than in England. Of course it is necessary to make allowance for the difference of customs, and for the different way of looking at things. Thus, to enter a mosque with dirty boots is not permitted—for the sufficient reason that the worshippers sit and prostrate themselves upon the floor—any more than would strangers with their hats upon their heads be suffered to walk about and talk in an English cathedral during divine service. For ladies to come unveiled into a mosque and stare about is as contrary to usage as it would be for Moslem women to enter an English church with their legs bare up to the knee. In the one case custom has ordained that it is indecent to uncover the face, in the other to uncover the ankles. But if a reasonable conformity to custom be observed, Christians in Cairo are more safe from insult or molestation than Mahommedans would be in many parts of London.

## III

## THE ENGLISH OCCUPATION.

IN conversing with Egyptians the subject of the English occupation has frequently come up. All my informants, with the exception of those of French or German nationality, regarded it as inevitable and beneficent. They acknowledged that for a long time to come Egypt will be unable to govern herself. A Pasha of Syrian origin thought that a governing element might be found among the Syrians of Beyrout, and an Armenian thought the same of his fellow-countrymen; but the Armenian objected to the Syrians, and the Syrian to the Armenians. The return of the Turk is not, however, desired. I asked whether, if the Sultan were to be driven from Constantinople, he would be welcomed in Cairo, and the answer was most decisively in the negative. Cairo, I was told, would be no place for him; let him go to Broussa, or, still better, to Damascus; but to Cairo, no. The spiritual office of the Khalif is looked upon in Egypt much as the office of the Pope is regarded in France. If he were attacked by a foreign Power, they would feel bound to defend him ; but they desire to have as little as possible of his presence or interference. "Would you," I asked, "welcome annexation by the English?" "Yes, if you would guarantee our debt, so that we might re-borrow at 3 per cent. and pay off the bondholders. The saving thus effected would make it possible to remit certain oppressive taxes, and would enable the government to be carried on with efficiency." It is the oppressive burden of the enormous debt which is the chief obstacle in the way of good administration. Although the higher posts are overmanned with Europeans drawing large salaries, the public departments are starved, the lower officials being so poorly paid that it is difficult to prevent them from taking bribes. The reduction of the burden of the debt, by the help of English credit, and above all the abolition of the Capitulations, which are no longer needed, and which render impossible the administration of equal justice, are, I was repeatedly told, the greatest blessings which England could confer on Egypt. But if these benefits were not secured, the Egyptians would prefer to be placed in the position of one of the protected feudatory States of India, guaranteed from all foreign interference, but left free to manage their own internal affairs in their own way. "But," I asked, "are any of these things within the range of practical politics?" "Perhaps not at present," was the reply, "but there was a grand opportunity which you missed. At the time of the bombardment of Alexandria you might have done anything you liked, and Europe would not have moved a finger; now, however, *c'est toute autre chose.* But the opportunity will arrive again; and take care that when it comes you are ready to take advantage of it. All that Egypt wants is tranquillity, freedom from foreign interference, and security from domestic disorder; and it is only the English who can give us that."

It is plainly seen in Cairo that if the English troops were to retire the immediate result would be intrigue and revolution, which might probably entail a French occupation, or the return of the Turks. If the English departed to-day, the Khedive, I was told, would have to go to-morrow, and his supporters the day after. "I doubt," said I, "whether the English Parliament would guarantee your debt, and perhaps without such a guarantee you would rather not be annexed." "Certainly not," was the reply. "Then there is nothing else but the continuance of the English occupation?" "It seems to be unavoidable." "How long will the English have to stay?" Most of those to whom I put this question thought that the occupation would have to be indefinite, as the fixing of a term would unsettle everything and destroy the present feeling of confidence, and retard the growing prosperity and wealth, the signs of which are everywhere manifest. When pressed to name a term, one Pasha considered that it might be possible to end the occupation in fifty years. Another mentioned fifteen years as the minimum limit; but this he thought was conditional on the possibility of a generation of honest Egyptian statesmen being raised up under English training to take the helm. I found no one who thought that the alternative of a French occupation would be preferable to an English protectorate. "We know," said one of the most intelligent Pashas, "that you English are honest and wish us well; but it would not be true—*ce serait un mensonge*— if I were to tell you that we love you. The French are *sympathiques*, you are not. I know all the English officials; there are not more than three or four" (and he told them off upon his fingers) "whom I can call my friends. You do not send us officials who understand us and our ways.

They are too imperious and meddle too much in small details. We are willing to be advised, but we do not like irritating interference. You are always making blunders. You have no fixed policy. As soon as a man learns to know the country he is removed." "Send us as few as possible, but as good as possible," said another Minister. "The Russians," one Pasha told me, "act more wisely than you do. They carefully pick the officers they send to Central Asia ; they send men who will be *bons camarades* with the natives. We do not like your officers—they are too haughty and too exclusive."

"Would it not be better," I said, "to send officials who have had an Indian training ? They, at all events, are acquainted with the customs of Mahommedan countries." "No," was the reply ; "we prefer those who come direct from England. It is true that you have sent us a few excellent Indian officers, especially some in the Departments of Public Works and Irrigation, but, as a rule, your old Indians are too imperious in their ways, and they think they have nothing to learn. Those who come from England accommodate themselves better to the country."

The same afternoon I had an illustration of the truth of these remarks. My informant was a

Mahommedan Pasha of great distinction ; a man of considerable culture, high position, with a large professional and private income ; better educated and informed than many an English gentleman, living in a charming house—a palace, I might call it—with numerous servants and all the appliances of Eastern luxury. Soon after reaching my hotel I received a visit from a young friend, who had recently joined his regiment. He was a nice frank English lad, fresh from a public school, where athletics had probably received more of his attention than any other branch of education. He had, I believe, crept into the army through the back-door of the militia ; his accomplishments were limited to cricket and lawn-tennis, his highest aspirations to snipe-shooting ; and his professional income consisted of his regulation pay of 5*s.* 3*d.* a day, supplemented, probably, by an allowance from the "governor." He knew nothing of Arabic, and a very little French. Only in one respect was he superior to my friend the Pasha ; he had the pink-and-white complexion of an English schoolboy, while the Pasha was nearly black. I told him of the visit from which I had just returned, and suggested that he should take opportunities of cultivating the society of some of the Egyptian gentlemen. "Gentlemen !" he said ; "you don't think I am going to call on any of those niggers. We conquered them, and they have got to behave accordingly. Call on those niggers! Not if I know it. If they want anything, it is their business to call on us." No wonder the wealthy, dignified, and accomplished Pasha complained of the English officers as being somewhat unsympathetic. If he had complained of their insolence and assumption, he would have been within the mark. My young friend, the sub-lieutenant, would have been totally incapable of following the brilliant political, literary, and scientific *causeries* of the " nigger " whom he so heartily despised.

I do not wish to imply that these two men are to be taken as representative types of their respective classes. The Pasha is a mature and exceptionally well-informed man, who by his own merits has reached the top of his profession, while the sub-lieutenant is merely an average English lad, not specially brilliant, who has all his steps to climb, and who will doubtless grow wiser as he grows older. But his conversation probably represents the ordinary tone of the mess-room. The moral I wish to convey is not that the average Egyptian is superior to the average Englishman—a proposition which would not be true—but that colour is no infallible test of intellect. And I think that the officers in command of the regiments quartered in Egypt would do well to ban the use of the offensive word " nigger," as applied to our allies. And to speak of Egypt as " a conquered country" is equally mischievous and absurd. We have all along been supporting a friendly sovereign against domestic revolution, and we have the high authority of the English Prime Minister who undertook the campaign for designating the Egyptian battles as merely " military operations," and not as " acts of war."

I am afraid that Tommy Atkins occasionally gives as much offence to the Cairo donkey-boys as his officers do to the Cairo Pashas. I once happened to witness a characteristic altercation. Thomas had partaken somewhat too freely of certain refreshments which are forbidden by the Koran, and, being in high spirits, thought that one of the " conquered people " should gratuitously supply a donkey for his use. The proprietor of the donkey did not see things in the same light, and considered that piastres would be a more satisfactory mode of settlement than fisticuffs. The Egyptian, unskilled in pugilistic science, retreated, satisfying himself with the Parthian shaft, " You' one big blackguard ! " The polyandrous habits of the English soldier also give offence to the pre-

judices of the Mahommedans ; and I was informed
that if there were to be any outbreak of fanaticism
in Cairo, the women of the town, whose existence
is largely due to the European element in the
population, would be the first victims of popular
fury.  Formerly most of these women were Italians;
but a demand creates a supply, and deep indignation is felt owing to Moslem women having adopted
a calling abhorrent to good Moslems.   In fact, the
grog shops and the houses of ill-fame are among
the chief reasons why the presence of European
soldiers is distasteful to the Egyptians of the lower
class.   A drunken soldier is pointed at in Cairo as
a drunken Helot was in Sparta.

For these, as well as for financial reasons, it
seems wise to restrict as much as practicable the
number of the occupying troops and to quarter the
bulk of them away from the great towns.

Doubtless there are reasons why the citadel
should be held by English troops, and there is a
manifest advantage in their being more or less in
evidence in such cities as Cairo and Alexandria.
But naturally the presence of foreign troops in
Cairo is not relished by the Egyptians: it is a
constantly visible sign of domination and sub-
jection, and the native outcry against the vices
imputed to them is in many cases merely the out-

ward expression of this dislike. But, on the whole, I do not think the British soldier is personally unpopular in Egypt. A great deal of coin is circulated by the army, and payment as a rule is liberal and prompt. I even think that the Egyptians of the lower class prefer the redcoats to the troops of their own nationality. In Upper Egypt I met with a curious illustration of the way in which English and native soldiers are regarded. At a large provincial town, where both English and native regiments had recently been stationed, I engaged an intelligent lad of fifteen to show me the way to the Mudir's house. As we went he told me that he had been employed as servant by an English officer, and had thus been constantly in and out of the barracks. I asked him which he liked best—the English soldier or the Egyptian soldier? "Me like English soldier best," he replied without hesitation. "Why?" "Because English soldier only beat Arab boy when him drunk; Egyptian soldier beat Arab boy always."

There can be no doubt that the English troops quartered in Cairo are a fine body of men, immeasurably superior to the Egyptian soldiers levied from among the fellaheen. The discipline is very strict; and, considering the climate and the temptations to which they are exposed, their conduct, on the whole, reflects credit on their officers and themselves. It would be absurd to represent them as anchorites, and of course in so large a number there are some black sheep ; but all the same I think the English officers are justly irritated by the sweeping accusations of immorality recently brought forward by Mr. Caine. There is too much immorality, no doubt : but, judging from the figures supplied to me by the Provost Marshal, I should say it had been exaggerated. Every effort is made to provide the men with rational amusements. There are clubs, reading-rooms, concerts, and amateur theatricals ; and if the soldier prefers the poisonous raki sold in the native grog-shops to the wholesome beverages supplied in the canteen, it is not the fault of his officers.

With regard to the preference expressed by one of my native informants for the French over the English, the Egyptians, I am told, know perfectly well that the athletic sports to which the young English officers are addicted keep them out of mischief. If the army of occupation were French instead of English, the subaltern officers, instead of occupying themselves with hunting, shooting, or lawn-tennis, would be playing dominoes in the cafés all day long with the natives, and in the evening would probably be intriguing with their wives.   The natives fully appreciate the difference, and know that with English officers the harem, at all events, is safe.   For obvious reasons, the younger officers are not encouraged by their superiors to form intimacies with the natives, and as a rule they keep apart.   The higher English officials say that the Beys and Pashas keep aloof from their society, and the latter retort that the English are haughty and unsympathetic.   Probably there is truth in both complaints.

There still survives, I find, a lively memory of the horrors which attended the French occupation under Bonaparte in 1798.   Denon in his travels gives a terrible picture of the scenes of massacre and violence which he witnessed.   The women of whole villages and towns were given up to brutal outrage, and I am told that in some places a distinct French type can be still recognized in the population.

# IV.

## BLACK OR WHITE.

I DO not think that the Egyptians are under any
delusion as to the value of the native army as a
fighting force. If any such delusions formerly
existed, they have been rudely dissipated. The
utter collapse of the Arabi bubble when pricked
by the British bayonet is an event too recent to
be easily forgotten ; and, in Cairo, at all events,
every one remembers the lesson of the memorable
hours that followed the Battle of Tel-el-Kebir.
Three of my friends—two of them Moslems, the
other a Maronite Christian—were among the
1500 adherents of the Khedive whose names were
on the list of those to be massacred if Arabi had
been victorious. One of them gave me a most
graphic account of their adventures during the
terrible days when the English were advancing
upon Cairo. I do not vouch for the facts, which
have doubtless been more accurately related by
correspondents who were with the English army ;

D

but I give the story as it was told me, as an
illustration of the way in which the dash and
courage of the English impressed the imagination
of Egyptians.  The three friends, knowing that
their names were on the list of the proscribed,
had purchased dromedaries, which they kept at a
village twelve miles out of Cairo, intending, at the
last moment, to make their escape across the
desert to the English army at Kosseir.  Through
those anxious days no news was allowed to reach
Cairo except through head-quarters ; and on the
afternoon of the day when the Battle of Tel-el-
Kebir was fought the report was spread that Arabi
had gained a great victory, and that the Duke of
Connaught and Lord Wolseley had been killed.
The next report was that these Generals and the
Khedive were prisoners, and were being brought
in triumph to Cairo, and it was announced that
Arabi and his victorious staff were about to arrive
by train.  Two of my friends went to the station
to see the arrival.  Arabi got out of the train with
a grey civilian coat over his uniform, and his
trousers covered with mud up to the knees ; and
then my friends first realized that he had been
defeated and that they were safe.  The next day
my friend drove out and met some English troopers ;
forty-eight of whom rode straight for the citadel,

demanded the keys from the commandant, who had judiciously retired to his bed, and took possession of the place without a shot being fired. There were 24,000 Egyptian troops in Cairo—8000 in the citadel and 16,000 at the Abbasiyeh Barracks—and on the appearance of the English cavalry they threw away their arms and fled helter-skelter each to his own village; turning their horses loose, so that there were hundreds galloping about the streets. My friend himself secured five, and numbers were being sold for a piastre or a couple of piastres each. Leaving a garrison of a dozen men at the citadel, the English assumed the command of the police and took possession of the railway station and the telegraph. The next day Lord Wolseley and his staff arrived, and all danger was over.*

My friend described the change in the city and in the demeanour of the people as something marvellous. Two days before, the adherents of

---

* The Cairo legend has, not unnaturally, exaggerated the disproportion of the numbers. I believe the intact Egyptian troops in the city did not amount to more than 10,000 men, 5000 of whom formed the garrison of the citadel. The Abbassiyeh barracks surrendered to an advanced guard of fifty troopers, while the detachment which took possession of the citadel consisted of one hundred and fifty. But I give the numbers as they were told me, since it is almost as important to know what well-informed Egyptians thought were the facts, as to know what they really were.

Arabi were walking ostentatiously about the streets, with their Korans in their hands, cursing the Christians and praying for a victory for the Egyptian army. As soon as the English arrived everything instantly became quiet ; and my friend assured me that most of the Moslems themselves were thankful for the result, having been forced to support the revolt against their will. If the cavalry had taken eight hours longer over their forced march, I am told that there would have been a frightful massacre, and the whole of the Frank quarter of Cairo would have been burnt. The spectacle of whole regiments of Egyptian soldiers giving up a strong fortress and throwing down their arms before a handful of English cavalry, contrasted with the promptitude, pluck, and daring of the English, made a deep impression on the inhabitants of Cairo. The Battle of Tel-el-Kebir itself probably had less moral effect than the capture of Cairo by the English cavalry.

Arabi's troops consisted largely of fellaheen conscripts from the Delta, who are constitutionally an unwarlike race. Whether they will ever supply good troops is doubtful, but there seems to be better material in the population of Upper Egypt. The black soldiers stationed at Assouan and Wady Halfa are spoken of as splendid troops, and

deeply attached to their English officers. Some
men of this race who were pointed out to me, I
could not help admiring. They were magnificent
animals, splendid savages of immense physical
strength and reckless daring, who, man for man,
in hand-to-hand conflict, equally well armed and
commanded, would probably overcome, by sheer
weight and strength and intrepidity, any other
soldiers in the world. Comparing them with the
half-grown town lads I have seen in our own
regiments, it was easy to understand how the
gigantic Goths and Burgundians bore down the
Roman legionaries; and it was impossible to avoid
the thought that if General Hicks's defeat had
been repeated at Abou Klea, and the magazines
and armouries of Egypt had fallen into the hands
of the Mahdi, civilization might have been exposed
to a flood of barbarism not less terrible than the
invasion of the Huns and Vandals who over-
whelmed the Roman empire, or of those hordes
of Turks or Mongols who in later times desolated
some of the fairest regions of the earth. Fortunately, however, for Egypt and for civilization, our
arms of precision and the steadiness of our troops
enabled us again and again to beat the Soudanese,
and one of the greatest dangers of modern times
has been averted. But it is possible that the

next great peril to civilization may come, not from the apprehended flood of Russian barbarism, but from the wild tribes of the Soudan. Egypt has more than once been conquered by Ethiopia; and who, in the seventh century of our era, would have anticipated that in a single generation the semi-barbarous tribes of Arabia would overthrow the ancient monarchy of Persia, and wrest some of its wealthiest provinces from the empire of Rome, extending their dominion in less than a century from the Indus to the Atlantic?

# V.

## POLYGAMY.

I WAS surprised to find that the "polygamous Moslem," of whom we hear so much in England, is practically non-existent in Mahommedan Egypt. Egypt has reached a point at which polygamy is rapidly becoming an anachronism. Among the labouring classes it is quite exceptional, for the sufficient reason that one wife is as much as a poor man can afford to keep. Among the higher classes I was prepared to find that many availed themselves of their privilege as Moslems, and followed the example of the Prophet ; but I was told that even among wealthy Pashas polygamy is becoming rare. "I know all, or nearly all, of the Pashas in Cairo," said one of my informants ; "and it would not be too much to say that 95 per cent. of them have only one wife." Seeing that I was somewhat incredulous, my friend took a sheet of paper and wrote down the names of all the principal Mahommedans in Cairo, beginning with the Khedive and the members of his family, and going through the various public offices. Of the whole number of Pashas and Beys with whom he was acquainted—and the list filled five pages—it appeared that all but two were strict monogamists. Of the two exceptions, in one case the first wife had failed to produce an heir, and at her request, and, as I understood, by her selection, a second wife had been installed in the harem. The other exception was a Turk of the old school, of whom my friend spoke in terms of disgust, such as we should use in speaking of Old Q. or of the profligates of the period of the Restoration. In India, also, polygamy has almost disappeared among the Moslems, less than 5 per cent. being polygamists; while in Persia, according to General Macgregor, the proportion amounts to only 2 per cent. of the population.

One cause which has tended to produce this result is the expense and inconvenience of the separate establishments that are required; but among the more religious Moslems the difficulty is felt that it is practically impossible to comply with the precepts of the Koran, which allows plurality of wives only on the condition that the husband shall treat them all with perfect equality, accord them the same privileges of every kind, and regard them with precisely the same affection. " C'est impossible d'être juste à quatre femmes," said one of my friends, a pious Moslem, explaining why he had only one wife.

It is a common assertion among Christian writers that Islam is unchangeable, immutable, incapable of development ; or, as Canon MacColl puts it, that " any progress beyond the Koran is not only superfluous, but impious in addition." How far this is from being the case is shown by the statements of Mahommedan jurists. They allege that in the early days of Islam, polygamy was necessary to preserve women from starvation or absolute destitution. But, they say, " in those Mahommedan countries where the circumstances which made its existence at first necessary are disappearing, plurality of wives has come to be regarded as an evil, and as something opposed to the teachings of the Prophet." " The conviction is gradually forcing itself on all sides in all advanced Moslem communities that polygamy is as much opposed to the Islamic laws as it is to the general progress of society and true culture. In India especially this idea is becoming a strong moral conviction, and many circumstances, in combination with this growing feeling, are tending to root out the existence of polygamy among the Mussulmans."

With regard to Egypt, all the Mahommedans with whom I conversed were, without exception, in favour of the legal prohibition of polygamy. "It is no part of our religion," said one of my friends; "it is permitted by the Koran under restrictions which are practically impossible to fulfil, but it is not ordained, and there would be no impiety in prohibiting it." One gentleman, a lawyer, was of opinion that, as in the case of slavery, which is also permitted in the Koran, a civil ordinance would suffice. "The Khedive," he said, "could to-morrow issue an ordinance making polygamy unlawful for the future; and if he were to do so, it would be accepted without serious objection." Several English officials to whom I submitted this opinion considered that such a step would be too great a risk, as it would be supposed that it was done at our instigation, and they thought that it could only be effected, without disturbance, by a decree of the Ulema. This is also the opinion of another Mahommedan lawyer, who writes, "it is earnestly to be hoped that before long a general synod of Moslem doctors will authoritatively declare that polygamy, like slavery, is abhorrent to the laws of Islam."

In India, however, the desired result has been attained in another way. A custom has grown up among Moslems that marriage deeds should contain a formal renunciation by the husband of the right to contract a second marriage during the existence of the first.

Another reproach commonly alleged against Islam is the facility and frequency of divorce. Mahommedans are as keenly alive to the evil as we are. " C'est la plus mauvaise chose possible," said the Mudir of a large province. The legal facilities for divorce exist, but the practical mischief is not so great as might be supposed. Among the upper and middle classes, public opinion is a sufficient restraint. It is considered disreputable to divorce a wife, so much so, that no father will give a daughter in marriage to a man who has disgraced himself by divorcing a wife for insufficient cause. In addition to considerations of family honour, another great security is the necessity imposed by Mahommedan law of restoring the divorced wife's dowry, which it is seldom convenient to do. No marriage is valid without an antenuptial settlement by the husband in favour of the wife. If the husband divorces her, he has to liquidate any portion of this sum which has not been already placed at her disposal. In some countries, such as India, these settlements are made so large as to be prohibitory of divorce.

But among the poorer classes divorce is common. Dowries are small, and the dowry of the first wife is repaid from that of the second. But here also, I was told, a simple regulation would suffice to reduce the number of divorces within very small limits. The fee paid to the cadi for pronouncing the sentence of divorce is at present only five piastres; if by a decree of the Khedive the fee were raised to as many pounds, the husband would think twice of the matter, and before he had got together the requisite sum there would be time for reconciliation. The increase of the fee and the diminution of the trouble would reconcile the cadis to the change. Thus it would be possible. without any overt interference with religion, to bring the marital relations of Mahommedans into accord with those which prevail in Western lands. In India, this result has already been practically attained, and divorce, even among the lower classes, is now so rare as to be inappreciable in its influence on public morality.

But so long as social customs make it impossible for the husband to obtain before marriage any sufficient knowledge of his intended wife's character and disposition, unhappy unions must be numerous, and to make the bond dissoluble only for the same causes as in England is not to be wished.

But the force of public opinion, together with a considerable indirect pecuniary penalty, may not improbably bring about the desired result.

The facility with which a legal divorce can be obtained has at all events one compensating advantage. The vernacular newspapers are absolutely free from those contaminating reports of divorce cases which disgrace the English press. Divorces, when they occur, do not become matters of common conversation. Mahommedan society is also free from the scandalous gossip relating to the reputation of women which is so common in the West. The nuisance of a "society paper" could not exist; such a journal would be starved for want of aliment. In Mahommedan society, the subject of women is tabooed. Whenever a number of young Englishmen or Frenchmen are gathered together, the ladies are sure to form a chief topic of conversation; but I am informed on good authority that, in *cafés* and other places to which young men resort in Cairo, it would be considered most improper to introduce such a subject. The home is more sacred in the East than in the West; and I think it may even be affirmed not only that there is less scandal, but even less occasion for it.

"Is not adultery punishable by death?" I asked, "Yes, by Mahommedan law; but it is not permitted by the law of Egypt." "I have heard," I said, "that unfaithful wives are put to death by their relations." "Yes, this happens sometimes; but in Egypt the inquiry into the causes of death is even more strict than your coroner's inquest in England, and such murders are very rare." My informant, a Pasha in the police service, thought that about one-third of the murders in Egypt might be due to this cause. Pressed further, he said the number might be between thirty and forty every year for the whole of Egypt. He based this estimate on the number of bodies of women with their throats cut found floating in the Nile. These deaths could hardly be called murders, he said; they were rather private executions decreed by family law. The knowledge of the penalty has a powerful deterrent effect, and my informant seemed to think that conjugal infidelity is rare.

The profligacy which is so commonly believed in England to characterize Mahommedans was indignantly denied by all my informants, Christians as well as Moslems. The lives of Moslem gentlemen are quite as decent and respectable, I was assured, as those of Englishmen. A Pasha of English birth, who is at the head of one of the great departments of State, told me he had lived for many years in the most intimate daily com-

panionship with Mahommedan gentlemen—officers
in the same Indian regiment with himself—and he
assured me that their lives were beyond reproach.

Calling on a Pasha who, from the office he holds,
has ample opportunities of knowing the facts,
I showed him the report of a sermon by an
English Prelate, holding up to detestation "the
depravity—indescribable, unutterable, unthinkable
—which had gone with Mahommedanism wherever
it had gone," and I asked him how much truth
there might be in such assertions. Being an
Eastern Christian, my friend had no bias in favour
of Mahommedanism, but he was most indignant
that such charges should be made, and he authorized me to deny them in the most explicit manner
possible. He assured me that there was less vice
in Cairo than in London, Paris, or Vienna—cities
which he knew well. A Mahommedan Pasha then
joined us, and, on being appealed to, said that
thirty or forty years ago there might have been
some small foundation for such accusations, but
that at the present time they were not true. He
added that by Mahommedan law the indescribable depravities alluded to were punishable by
death. While we were talking, a Russian gentleman, who holds a diplomatic appointment at
Bokhara, dropped in, and, as regards that country,

confirmed what had been said. He added that, just before he left Bokhara, a man and his wife had been executed for the crime of permitting their daughter to form an immoral connection with a wealthy person. As for the assertion that Moslem colleges are dens of profligacy, he said that, as regards the five or six large colleges at Bokhara, it was absolutely false. In the Government colleges at Cairo, where there are 3000 boarders of all ages up to twenty-five, the least suspicion of immorality is followed by immediate expulsion, and during the last three years only four students have been expelled.

The subject is an unpleasant one; but I have thought it a duty to put these statements on record, and I may add that all my informants were persons of position, with ample opportunities for knowing the facts, and that they seemed to me to be manifestly sincere.

# VI.

## THE HAREM.

In England the very name of the harem is a term of reproach. At the *table d'hôte*, I was sitting next to a fellow-countrywoman, a lady of unusual intelligence and culture. I ventured to tell her that my wife had recently visited a Mahommedan harem. The information greatly shocked her feelings of propriety, and she said that nothing would ever induce *her* to visit such an improper place. She was surprised to learn that harems are not "dens of profligacy and infamy," but merely the ladies' apartments in an Eastern house. The relations between the master of the harem and its inmates are no more necessarily immoral than those between the head of an English family and the servants in his establishment. The lady to whom the visit had been paid had been a Circassian slave in the harem of the Khedive, who had given her in marriage to my friend as a mark of his esteem ; but the Khedive is faithful

E

to his wife, and no more " infamy " attached to such a marriage than would attach in England to a marriage between a maid of honour and a lord-in-waiting.

As to the large number of women who reside in some Oriental harems, a very simple and obvious explanation was given me. Every Mahommedan gentleman is bound in honour to receive into his harem his own female relatives, and also the female relatives of his wife, if they are in need of a protector, and these ladies, like Englishwomen of the same rank, require numerous attendants to wait upon them, and ladies in Egypt are quite as particular as in England about the characters of their servants.

As to concubinage between the master and the female servants in the harem, the latter, I was told, would be the least likely to object, as they might thereby gain a permanent position in the household; but this the master would be as unwilling to accord, since a female servant who bears a child to her master cannot be dismissed, and the child is frequently legitimated by a subsequent marriage, and, in default of other heirs, inherits the whole or a portion of the family property. The mother of the Khedive, a woman universally beloved for her charity and goodness of heart, formerly occupied a menial position in the service of the late Khedive. He took a fancy to her, and married her; but her lowly origin has been no reproach, and the duty and affection shown to her by the present Khedive was the subject of universal panegyric. I am told that his Court is as blameless as that of St. James's; and that in all the relations of life he sets an admirable example to his subjects.

A Mahommedan gentleman, who probably knows as much of the institutions of his co-religionists as Western writers, describes the harem as " the sanctuary of conjugal happiness. It is prohibited to strangers because of the reverence accorded to women. In the harem the wife reigns supreme. The husband has no authority within that circle."

The seclusion of women and the veil are social proprieties rendered necessary for the present by the low standard of education among women, and by the want of early opportunities for mixing in society. They are Oriental customs rather than Mahommedan institutions. They formerly prevailed among Eastern Christians, but are gradually being abandoned. An Egyptian Bey, himself a Maronite Christian, told me that his own grandfather had never seen his wife's face before he married her. His mother, he said, never went into gentlemen's society. He himself was married to an Irish lady, who of course enjoyed the social freedom usual in Western lands. Here was an instance of the manner in which, in three generations, an Eastern family had gradually emancipated itself from the restrictions of Oriental custom. The example thus set by Syrians and Armenians will doubtless be followed. The veil of Mahommedan ladies in high position is becoming almost as transparent as the veils worn by English ladies in Hyde Park, and the emancipation of women from undue social restraints is undoubtedly only a question of time. The way in which American girls dispense with chaperons, and even travel alone by railway, is as shocking to French or Italian notions of propriety as the low dresses of English ladies are to Mahommedans. To call a harem a "den of infamy" is about as accurate as it would be for a Mahommedan to apply the same description to an English ball-room.

From all that I could learn, I do not think that women are themselves discontented with the present domestic system. The veil is not a disadvantage, and women would be the last to wish it to be abolished, since it gives them great freedom of locomotion. I was told that if a man were to meet his own wife in the street he would be bound to pass her without recognition, and would not dream of accosting her or of lifting her veil. She would be at once protected from such an outrage by the indignation of the bystanders. Since under the protection of the veil a woman can go anywhere without remark, delicate matters of business are largely in their hands. If any official desires promotion, or wishes to arrange a difficult affair, he usually confides the matter to his wife, who is able secretly to visit the wife of the man in power.

Undoubtedly the want of facilities for female education is one of the greatest hindrances in the way of the relaxation of existing restrictions. The Protestant mission schools do not find much favour, as parents are not unreasonably afraid of proselytism; while "emancipated" women have the same difficulty in finding husbands in Egypt as in England, and for similar reasons. Schools for young ladies have, however, been instituted by the Khedive, and English or Swiss governesses are not unfrequently employed in Eastern families.

As to the intelligence of Egyptian women, it is difficult for a foreigner to form any opinion. I may say, however, that in the primary mixed schools for young children which I visited the girls seemed to be in no way behind the boys. I had also the privilege of being admitted to the *salon* of an Egyptian lady of high rank, and of discussing freely with her the position of women in the East. She had been educated by an English governess, and I found her in manners and intelligence quite the equal of her European sisters. She was well read and well informed, acquainted with current European literature and European politics, and in London or Paris would take rank as a distinguished ornament of the best society.

Even among the lower and middle classes the bonds of custom are being broken through. I was taken by the superintending Pasha to see a school where a number of young women were being trained as midwives. I was greatly pleased with their intelligence, and still more with their demeanour. There was no giggling or curiosity at the presence of male visitors, and they answered the questions put to them without shyness, but with natural grace and perfect modesty. These girls wear veils in the streets, but are allowed to dispense with them within the walls of the college. The superintendent, a young Mahommedan lady, reminded me, in dress and demeanour, of a " sister " or " mother superior " at one of our London hospitals.

# VII.

## EGYPT FOR THE EGYPTIANS.

A FEW weeks spent in Upper Egypt have given me an opportunity of testing by personal observation the correctness of certain statements made by the Cairo Pashas. I have also been furnished with letters of introduction to the Mudirs of several provinces, some of whom are men of intelligence and cultivation, others the reverse.

I came to Egypt with the expectation of finding that the English administration had been an unmixed blessing to the country, and that the evils produced by centuries of misgovernment were being rapidly remedied by beneficent reforms introduced by English statesmen. And no doubt much good has been done. In Upper Egypt especially one notes everywhere the signs of increasing security and prosperity. The fellaheen are no longer openly plundered by Government officials; flagrant oppressions are impossible; the peasant knows that when the legal taxes have been paid he is free from all further demands. The taxes seem heavy, but they are mostly in the nature of rents and irrigation rates, rather than what in England would be called taxes. But in other matters it may be doubted whether the blessings of English rule are appreciated. We have probably gone in advance of native opinion, and have run counter to immemorial custom. The people are used to personal government, and submit to it. We have undermined the authority of the Mudirs (the native governors of provinces) without substituting for it anything which the people can understand. A form of government theoretically open to objection produces better practical results, if decently administered, than institutions excellent in theory but unworkable in practice. The Mudirs were local despots, but not necessarily tyrants: for fear lest they should abuse their powers we have so tied their hands with the red tape of a central bureaucracy as to impair their means of beneficent action.* Everything has

* I am indebted to a distinguished Egyptian official for the following observations: "There is a fundamental difference between Eastern and Western methods of bureaucratic Government. In Western countries there are central administrations which extend their branches to the provinces, the local administrators being controlled from the capital. In the East, all departments of Government are, in each province, centralized under a single head, who holds the threads of the various administrations. In Egypt

. to be referred to Cairo, and the instructions
received are often contradictory or impossible.
The wiser course would have been to select better
men for the office of Mudir, and to invest them
with a fuller responsibility. For a long time to
come personal government will be a necessity in
Egypt. We should have aimed at getting good
personalities instead of making government im-
personal.

It is the same with the village sheikhs,
who are answerable for the good order of the
villages they govern and for the payment of the
taxes. Formerly the office was eagerly sought
by local magnates; but we have deprived the
sheikhs of those prerogatives of their office which
they most valued, and have left them only the

these local heads are the Mudirs. Our reforms have tended to
emancipate the local officials from the authority of the Mudirs, and
to give them their orders direct from the Englishmen who control the
central administrations at Cairo. Thus the Mudirs see their old
power and prestige passing away, and their subordinates take
pleasure in ' regretting that their orders from Cairo will not permit
them to comply' with the directions of their nominal chiefs. The
Mudirs, however, are biding their time; and when we leave Egypt,
the tendency to reaction will be aggravated by their resentment, and
the ignorance of details which we have fostered. Our system may
produce the most rapid results, but it will be destroyed the moment
our backs are turned. It would be wiser to adopt the slower but
surer method of instructing those into whose hands the administration of the country will eventually fall, and *through them* con-
veying all orders to those who will then become their subordinates."

more invidious and unpleasant duties, so that it is becoming increasingly difficult to induce men of local influence and position to accept thankless offices.   Duty and privilege should go together. Fearing lest privileges should be abused, we have taken them away, and are then surprised to find a reluctance to discharge the unpleasant duties which we have left.   Mommsen has well shown in his two last volumes that the same blunder was the ruin of the Roman provincial administration. The duties of the unpaid local administrators were made so odious and onerous, that there was a general desire on the part of men of position to escape burdens which at an earlier time were associated with privileges which caused them to be readily undertaken or even to be eagerly sought.   A Local Government Bill in England which would make the chief landed proprietors unwilling to undertake the duties of local administration—thereby lowering the *personnel* of quarter sessions down to the level of boards of guardians —would be a calamity; and this is the very blunder we are likely to commit in Egypt.

The good government of Egypt depends, to an extent which in England we can hardly realize, on the character of the Mudirs.   Personal government is plainly a necessity; a visible accessible autocrat is the only thing the people understand. They are docile, even servile ; illegal orders of the Mudir, or of the village sheikh, are obeyed without expostulation. The fellaheen themselves supply no elements for local self-government ; they seem to have no patriotism, no aspirations, no public spirit, no disposition to resist tyrannies, hardly anything that can be called a feeling of nationality. I see no prospect, immediate or remote, of any really national Government in Egypt. I could not hear of a single native Egyptian, of pure Copt or fellah blood, who occupies high office or is considered capable of filling it. The Egyptian Pashas are all of foreign extraction, Turks, Circassians, Armenians, Syrians, Jews, Arabs, or Berberines. Their families may have been domiciled in Egypt for generations ; but, though Orientals, undistinguishable in dress or manners from the Egyptians, they are almost as much foreigners as we are ourselves. Since the first Assyrian conquest, certainly since the time of Cambyses, no Egyptian dynasty has ruled in Egypt ; for six and thirty centuries the Egyptians have submitted with docility to alien domination. Foreigners—either Ethiopians, Assyrians, Babylonians, Persians, Greeks, Romans, Arabs, Saracens Circassians, Turks, or Arnauts—have ruled in

Egypt; but Egyptians never.   The English supremacy is the last in the long list, and not the least beneficent.   If we were to go, the alternative would be a period of anarchy, followed probably by the return of the Turks or by a French occupation; and it is difficult to say which would be the least disastrous for the Egyptians.   To withdraw now, when our reforms, as I shall presently show, have made impossible the old methods of administration, would be nothing less than a crime.

This proved incapacity of the Egyptians for self-government has to be accounted for.   The native Egyptians—Copts or fellaheen—are by no means deficient in ability of a sort.   In going over the schools and colleges in Cairo I was astonished to find the pupils brighter and more intelligent than English lads of the same age.   It is the same in the village schools—the children are wonderfully sharp and quick, exhibiting none of the loutish stolidity of English village lads.   The boys in the streets pick up English from travellers with surprising rapidity, and no London *gamins* could surpass them in the dexterous ingenuity with which they divine and supply the wants of passers-by.   The young men in the colleges at Cairo learn quickly, and produce their knowledge with facile rapidity.   But precocious as they are, especially in languages and mathematics, they are never much more than grown-up children. It is only the sons of naturalized Egyptians of foreign extraction—Turks, Circassians, Greeks, or Syrians—who seem to be capable of the higher culture.

The fact is universally admitted, but the explanation is not so easy. I have talked with several Englishmen who have had under them large numbers of Egyptian subordinates, and they all seemed to think that it was hopeless to attempt to train native Egyptians for any of the higher administrative posts. They have no continuous energy, they are merely imitative, possessing no power of origination. I believe that no book of original research has ever been written by an Egyptian. The vernacular press is mainly in the hands of Syrians. In the colleges the students are apt at bookwork, but less skilful in the solution of problems. An English official who had numerous Egyptian clerks in his office admitted the precocious cleverness of the boys, but asserted that the early promise of their youth was invariably unfulfilled. He attributed the deterioration to the habitual misuse of narcotics—opium, hashish, or tobacco; but a Levantine Pasha, to whom I offered this explanation, said that it was not sufficient, as the want of energy and initiative was noticeable among Egyptians who did not use these drugs, which did not similarly affect Orientals domiciled in Egypt. I have reluctantly come to the conclusion that it is largely a question of race, and possibly to some extent of climate. The native Egyptian, like the Bengalee Baboo, is clever, imitative, and assimilative; but is without the practical faculty of rule which is found in the Sikh, the Mahratta, the Arab, or the Turk.

Together with this inherent want of power, of force of character, which makes the cry of Egypt for the Egyptians a Utopian dream, we have the difficulty arising from the early maturity and early decline of the race. The men, like the women, develop all their powers prematurely—an unnatural development which is followed by a premature decay. The girls are marriageable at twelve, are mothers at thirteen, and old women at twenty-five. The boys are men at fifteen and worn out at thirty-five—an age at which an Egyptian official is as much past useful work as an Englishman at sixty. It is plain that the Egyptians are not a governing or ruling race. Although inheriting the oldest civilization in the world, they have been for 3000 years a conquered and not a conquering people. If the English were to retire, I am afraid it must be confessed that the best hope for Egypt would be government by the "inhuman species of humanity"—the descendants of those unspeakable Turks to whom we are so largely compelled to look for occupants of the higher military and administrative posts.

# VIII.

## THE KOURBASH.

THE Reforms which we have initiated make the continuance of English rule more necessary than ever. The Turkish and Levantine Pashas by whose aid we are now governing Egypt are as yet unable to go alone, as we have impulsively abolished the only method of rule with which they were familiar. The *kourbash*, for instance, is a time-honoured Egyptian institution, as ancient as the Pyramids. The whip and the stick appear in the paintings in some of the oldest Egyptian tombs. On Western principles it is indefensible to use a stick for extracting taxes from unwilling taxpayers, or true testimony from reluctant witnesses; and the total and immediate abolition of the legal use of the kourbash is perhaps the greatest of the "reforms" we have introduced in Egypt. But though we have made it illegal we have not abolished it. We have so far abolished it as to increase the difficulties of administration;

but a custom which has prevailed for five thousand years cannot be stopped instantaneously by an edict. The traveller's guide, dragoman, or donkey-boy, the guardian of a tomb or temple, the village policeman—in short, any one in a position of real or assumed authority—clears the way through the crowd by the good-humoured application of a whip, applied, it is true, to the flowing skirts of the clothing of the natives rather than to the back; and I have even seen an ardent English Radical, throwing to the winds the principles of the *Daily News*, clear for himself the necessary passage by the totally illegal application of a "brutal and degrading punishment," ineffectively administered with his umbrella.

All the Egyptians to whom I have spoken on the subject, whether Pashas or peasants, think the total abolition of the kourbash was one of our mistakes. The Pashas think so because it has made government more difficult; the peasants because it has made government more harsh. Of this the other day I had an amusing illustration. My dragoman, or donkey-boy—for he acted in both capacities—is a well-to-do respectable married man of about forty. He came to me one evening after dinner. "My master, you want me to-morrow? My brother Hassan, all same me, go along you." "Well, Mahomet," I said, "I don't mind taking Hassan to-morrow; but why can't you go yourself, as usual?" "Me got plenty business to-morrow—very 'ticlar business. Me not go to-morrow if my master not mind." "Well, what sort of business is it that is so particular?" "Me want to go to prison." It seems that for some "contravention," as it is called—allowing his donkeys to stand at some forbidden spot off the "rank"—Mahomet had been fined sixty piastres, with the alternative of two days' imprisonment. If I would consent to take his brother Hassan, "all same me," he would prefer to go to prison and save the piastres; but rather than let the job go out of the family he would pay the money. I agreed to the imprisonment, and when he came out I asked him about the old times. He would then, he said, have had a dozen strokes of the kourbash, and the whole business would have been over in ten minutes. He preferred the kourbash to either the fine or the prison; where, however, the chief hardships were that smoking was forbidden and fleas were unduly numerous. However, his wife insisted on the piastres being saved, if possible, and she rewarded her good man's compliance by taking to him in prison the best dinner he had eaten for many weeks.

The ultimate abolition of the kourbash was inevitable, and will in time prove to be a beneficent reform. But its sudden and total prohibition by Lord Dufferin was a hazardous experiment, and it might have been wiser to have begun by restricting its use at first to grave offences, and by limiting the number of strokes that could be legally inflicted. Even the Egyptian peasant, as I have shown, regards its abolition as a very doubtful blessing. Of course he did not like it, but the necessary substitute he likes even less. Give him his choice, and an English schoolboy prefers a flogging to the loss of a half-holiday; it hurts him less, and he prides himself on his manliness in bearing it. It is much the same with the Egyptians, who do not entirely appreciate our sentimental objections to one of the immemorial institutions of the country. In the old days a fellah with plenty of money thought himself bound to take a certain number of strokes before paying his taxes; and I am told that if he paid down forthwith his wife would usually administer the stick herself, to mark her opinion of her husband's want of proper feelings of frugality and courage.

The Egyptians seem to have no sense of personal rights, and no notion of resistance to the tyranny of an official, or a person in any position of quasi-authority. I was the other day the unwilling witness of an outrage which is curiously characteristic of this submissiveness of the Egyptian character. An old man, grey-headed, arrived as a passenger on one of the Government postal steamers. In disembarking, encumbered with his prayer-carpet and sleeping-rug, and evidently somewhat enfeebled by years, he was not sufficiently alert to satisfy the *reis*, who wanted to clear the vessel. The *reis* took up a deck-stool and hurled it at the old man, felling him to the ground with a wound in the temple which bled profusely. The *reis* expressed no concern, made no apology, and offered no assistance. The bystanders most humanely assisted the sufferer, carried him on shore, washed his face, and bathed the wound ; one of them most judiciously placing his finger on the ruptured blood-vessel to stop the bleeding. But no one in the crowd expressed the slightest indignation at the outrage, or even remonstrated with the offender ; and, as far as I could learn, no intention of appealing to the police was entertained.

An Englishman holding a high office told me, however, a story which indicates the possibility of the growth of a feeling which may make Egyptian freedom ultimately more possible. A Mudir not long ago ordered a fellah, I think

because he refused to give evidence, to lie down
and submit to the kourbash. " No," said the man,
"you cannot do that now, because the English are
in Egypt, and I shall complain." The Mudir was
cowed and revoked his order. This, I must confess, is about the most hopeful story I have heard.
It shows that the fellaheen are learning to know
their position and to insist upon their legal rights.
But the abolition of the kourbash, without the
substitution of something else in its place, has
occasioned some curious complications. Thus I
am informed that by the law of Egypt a man cannot be executed, even for murder, unless three
conditions are fulfilled. The warrant must issue
from the Government; the family of the murdered
man must demand it; and the justice of the judicial
decision must be ratified by the confession of the
criminal. The connivance of the injured party
can frequently be secured by a liberal administration of backsheesh; but the confession of the
accused could only be obtained by the use of the
kourbash. But now that the kourbash is abolished
confessions are not forthcoming, and the most
atrocious crimes remain unpunished, as the
sentence of death cannot legally be inflicted.

# IX.

## THE CORVÉE.

WHAT has just been said about the kourbash applies also to other innovations which we have introduced. From an English point of view they may be desirable reforms; but in many cases the changes are in advance of native opinion, and are opposed to immemorial custom. With the best intentions we are in danger of going too fast. Western ideas are difficult to engraft on Oriental institutions. The abolition of the *corvée*, on which we greatly pride ourselves, affords one of the best illustrations of the mistaken or overhasty application of Western notions to an Eastern country. For five thousand years it has been a fundamental institution in Egypt. The vast canals and irrigation works, to which Egypt has owed her past prosperity and wealth, are due to the *corvée*. Without it, such works could not have been constructed or maintained. Forced labour of any kind may be represented as a modified form of

slavery, and the *corvée* has consequently been
denounced in England as an intolerable oppression.
Doubtless, it is most objectionable in principle ;
but, when we come to practice, its total abolition
would entail great evils, and if freed from abuse
it is beneficent and equitable, and even necessary.
When the Nile rises, and the dykes require suddenly to be strengthened, thousands of labourers
are required all at once and at short notice.   The
work is in the direct interest of the fellaheen ; it
is their own crops which have to be saved.   In
old times the whole population could be called
out by the Mudir to perform the work, which
was done rapidly and effectively.   No objection
was made ; the necessity and the advantage were
self-evident.   It was forced labour, no doubt ;
but the inequity would lie in permitting any one
to be exempt from it.   The fellaheen see this ;
forced labour, in such a case, merely means that
the idle and selfish shall not be allowed to shirk
the necessary duty of labouring, at an emergency,
for the common benefit.   It would be a far greater
hardship for the work to be done by labour paid
for by a rate : the peasants, at most seasons, can
spare the labour better than the money.   Besides,
at a moment's notice contractors could not be
found to undertake the work, or even the money

to pay the labourers; and, if this difficulty could be overcome, there would be lavish expenditure, and much jobbery and corruption. To save a single district at the cost of the central treasury would be still more inequitable. Far better suited to the nature of the country and the habits of the people, is the time-honoured plan by which the sheikhs set the whole population to work, the district being saved in the shortest possible time and at the smallest cost. Regarded in the right light, the *corvée* is not, as asserted, a modified form of slavery, but an ancient application of the modern principle of beneficial mutual co-operative labour on a large scale.

Even in England, parish roads, not under a county highway board, are practically maintained by an equitable form of the *corvée*. A highway rate is laid, and the farmers are eager to work out their respective share of the rate by team labour, or by the services of their farm servants, in lieu of money payments.

Of course the *corvée* is liable to abuse, and beyond doubt it has been cruelly abused; but the sensible plan would be to remedy the abuses instead of doing away with a beneficent institution. The larger landowners, who benefit most by the works, should not, as hitherto, be exempt, but should pay a proportionate contribution; the population of whole villages should not be swept off to a distance from their homes, to work for the benefit of some wealthy landowner who is able to bribe the local authorities; and this, perhaps, at some critical season, when their harvest requires to be garnered, or when their own lands are parched, and it is essential that they should labour without intermission at the shadoof to save their crops from perishing for want of water. By all means remedy the abuses; but, because in times past serious abuses have prevailed, that is no reason why we should impulsively uproot and destroy a system eminently adapted to the country and the people.

Mr. Gladstone imagined that the *corvée* was a sort of Hebrew bondage, a tyranny too terrible to be borne; and our administrators pride themselves on the steps they are taking to destroy an arrangement to which Egypt owes that great part of her wealth and fertility which arises from a vast system of public works of irrigation—canals, dams, or embankments—executed many of them in the times of the old Egyptian Empire, which have to be repaired and maintained at a great expenditure in labour. The objections to the *corvée* are mainly sentimental rather than practical;

and the Egyptians themselves, who know where the shoe pinches better than we do, will not thank us for our blundering philanthropy in undertaking to abolish it.

The foregoing remarks about the *corvée* called forth the following letter, which I venture to reprint from the *St. James's Gazette* of February 17th.

"I was much interested in Canon Taylor's remarks about the *corvée* in Egypt. His views as to the inexpediency of abolishing the *corvée* are fully borne out by what has happened in India.

"In Southern India—and probably in the north also—there existed from time immemorial an institution called 'Kudi Marāmat,' or 'customary labour,' according to the laws of which the native peasantry or small farmers, with their servants or coolies, were compelled to undertake so much actual labour annually in the fields. This labour was directed to the upkeep of the tank or reservoir, with the supply, drainage, or irrigation channels connected therewith, or to the protective works— dykes, flood-banks, etc. In time of emergency, such as disastrous floods, this 'Kudi Marāmat' was found most useful, as under its agency compulsory labour was immediately brought to bear when required; it was custom, and no one grumbled, and everybody benefited more or less. Now this custom has been allowed to fall into abeyance year by year, partly through ignorance on the part of the English rulers, partly from mistaken philanthropy and the nonsense about 'slavery' and so forth which appears to have been the death of the *corvée* in Egypt.

"What is the result? All the minor irrigation works—and their name is legion—throughout Southern India have fallen into such a state of disrepair and ruin that to set them in order now is an impossibility, and, even if practicable so far as the required labour is concerned, would be utterly beyond the means of the State financially. All this waste and all this ruin has been brought about by the want of the 'stitch in time' which the 'Kudi Marāmat' so easily and so continuously provided. The ryots have been so pampered by our kind rule, that they look to the State to cure all their ills and do all their repairs for them; and they have lost all idea of self-help in these matters since their only safeguard—their only means of co-operation—the old 'Kudi Marāmat,' has become a thing of the past; and universal decay is the consequence.

"An experience of some twenty-five years on the irrigation works of Southern India enables me to state the above as a fact, and no exaggeration.

Some four or five years ago an effort was made by the Madras Government, and more particularly by the practical engineer members, to revive the 'Kudi Marāmat' by special legislation ; but things had been improved so fast and so far by our beneficent rule that no stand could be made against the whisper, I will not say the cry, of ' revival of slavery.' I mention this to show how important the matter was considered. The engineers, however, were discomfited ; and the country goes on decaying in consequence. The present chief engineer in Madras would, I am sure, bear me out in all I say.

" This state of things cannot be known to the powers that be in England ; for, with such an example and warning before them, they would never have abolished the *corvée* in Egypt. Truly, misplaced and mistaken philanthropy has a deal to answer for."

# X.

## SLAVES.

NATURALLY on visiting for the first time a country where slavery prevails, I asked many questions on the subject. The answers I received certainly tended to put the matter in a somewhat different light from that in which it is regarded by ourselves. Slavery is indefensible on any principles recognized in England. It is the red rag which, waved in the face of John Bull, drives him into fury. But Mr. Froude has probably led a few of us to doubt whether the last state of Hayti or Jamaica is so very much better than the first, and whether a slower process than immediate emancipation might not have been more beneficent for the negro as well as less disastrous to the planter. It may be agreed that the evils inseparable from the slave-trade are so terrible that it should be peremptorily stopped ; but it is very doubtful whether either slaves or masters will be greatly benefited by the impending abolition of domestic slavery in Egypt.

In most cases the position of the slaves will be distinctly altered for the worse. They are subjected to no cruelties or hardships, and compulsory manumission will deprive them of the claim they now possess to a comfortable maintenance in their old age.

One of my informants told me that a near relation, one of the largest slave-owners in Egypt, had fourteen slaves, who were all aged, and practically useless, but had to be supported. When manumission comes this gentleman will be freed from all legal obligation towards them, though from a sense of duty he may probably still continue to maintain them. If slavery had been left alone and the slave-trade stopped, slavery, considering the present rate of voluntary manumission, would, in a few years, have become extinct in Egypt, without any of the impending hardships to the slaves.

As to the actual number of slaves now existing in Egypt, I was told that there might be as many as five hundred in Cairo, but that there were very few elsewhere. "Would it be possible," I asked, "to buy a slave?" "Yes, possible perhaps, but very difficult." In two or three years slavery will be legally abolished, but the abolition was hardly necessary, as under the present law

any slave can obtain his freedom if he chooses.
But very few claim it, because as a rule they are
much better off than if they were freed. They
are often wealthy; they are regarded as members
of the family, and occupy confidential positions in
the household. There is nothing that corresponds
to the slavery which recently existed in the United
States. No slaves are employed in field-labour :
they are rather in the position of the upper servants
in an English family. " Have you any slaves yourself?" I asked one gentleman. "I had one, who
was bequeathed to me by my father, but I freed him
and married him to my niece. It often happens
that a slave is married to his master's daughter,
and inherits the property if there are no other heirs."
"It seems a very curious arrangement," I said.
" Not at all," was the reply. " You know all about
the slave, you know his character better than you
would know the character of any other suitor ; the
family is not broken up, and the property is kept
together. All Moslems are regarded as brothers,
and the slave who marries a daughter of the house
continues to reside with the family as before, which
would not be the case with any other marriage.
It is a very convenient plan."

A generation ago, I was informed, slavery was
the surest road to wealth, honour, and position.

Edmond About, in his charming volume " Le Fellah," gives a list of some half-dozen of the then Egyptian Ministers who had been slaves ; and many of the leading families in Cairo at the present day are descended from slaves.   Even now slavery is no reproach, and the slaves whom I have seen were sleek and well clad, and did not appear to be discontented with their lot.   The English crusade against slavery is doubtless one cause of the complaint I have so often heard, that the English do not understand the Egyptians and their ways.   It is very possible ; and it is possible also that if a Mahommedan army was occupying London, some of our social institutions, such as the gin-palace and the dancing-saloon, might seem so objectionable that the Puritan party among the Moslems might clamour for their forcible suppression.

# XI.

## WINTER AT LUXOR.

For those who are driven into temporary exile by the rigours of an English winter, there is no spot which offers such advantages in the way of climate, combined with such unique attractions in accessible objects of historic interest, as Luxor, one of the four scattered villages which stand upon the site of Thebes. The ancient monuments are rivalled only by those of Rome and Athens; the winter climate is warmer and far healthier than that of Rome, while Athens can hardly be visited with comfort before the spring. January, the coldest month of the year, is like a calm, sunny English September; the thermometer indoors ranging from 61 deg. in the daytime to 58 deg. at night, while the barometer is steady at 31½ in. The fact that in neither of the two hotels, occupied largely by invalids, is there chimney or fireplace in any of the rooms, and that the only access to the bedrooms is by external galleries open to the night air, speaks sufficiently for the temperature; and the winter, if such it can be called, consists practically of three or four cloudy days, with possibly a slight clap of thunder, followed sometimes by a shower lasting for a few minutes. Umbrellas are necessary, but only as a protection against the sun, which is as brilliant as at Cannes or Nice, while the climate is far less treacherous; the dreaded mistral of Cannes, and the cold blasts which at Nice descend from the snow-clad Maritime Alps, being replaced by an occasional dust-storm from the Libyan desert. With all qualifications, the climate is drier, warmer, more bracing, and more equable than that of any other winter health-resort I know of.

This paradise for the invalid is now comparatively easy of access. A pleasant twelve days' voyage in one of the floating palaces owned by the Indian or Australian companies lands the traveller in Egypt at a cost not very greatly exceeding what would be paid for a residence of equal duration in a first-class hotel. The Bay of Biscay, it is true, is somewhat of a lottery; but nine times out of ten it may be crossed without serious discomfort, and when once Gibraltar is reached the traveller may expect a delicious voyage on an even keel over a summer sea. For those who dread the ocean, Egypt may be reached more expeditiously, though with greater discomfort and fatigue, by one of the overland routes, taking ship either at Brindisi, Naples, or Marseilles.

After a few days at Cairo—one of the most amusing and picturesque cities in the world—the Express Nile Service of Messrs. Cook brings the traveller in three days to Luxor, where he will find enough to occupy him for as many weeks. The first view from the river shows the appositeness of the epithet Hecatompylos, applied to Thebes by Homer. Huge cubical masses of masonry—not the gateways of the city, which was never walled, but the pylons and propylons of the numerous temples—are seen towering above the palms, and, separated from each other by miles of verdant plain, roughly indicate the limits of the ancient city.

At Luxor the Nile valley is about ten miles across. The escarpment of the desert plateau, which elsewhere forms a fringing cliff of nearly uniform elevation, here breaks into cone-shaped peaks rising to a height of seventeen hundred feet above the level plain, which in January is already waving with luxuriant crops—the barley coming into ear, the lentils and vetches in flower, and the tall sugar-canes beginning to turn yellow. The plain is dotted with Arab villages, each raised above the level of the inundation on its *tell*, or mound of ancient *débris*, and embosomed in a grove of date-palms mingled with the quaint dom-palms characteristic of the Thebaid.   Animal life is far more abundant than in Italy or France.   We note the camels and buffaloes feeding everywhere, tethered in the fields; the great soaring kites floating in the air; the graceful hoopoes which take the place of our English thrushes; the white paddy-birds fishing on the sand-banks in the river; gay kingfishers, among them the fish-tiger pied in black and white; the sun-bird, a bee-eater clad in a brilliant coat of green and gold; the crested lark, the greater and lesser owl, as well as water-wagtails, pipits, chats, and warblers, numerous swifts and swallows, with an occasional vulture, eagle, cormorant, pelican, or crane.   The jackal is common; and the wolf, the hyæna, and the fox are not unfrequently heard, but seldom seen.

The sunsets on the Nile, if not the finest in the world, are unique in character.   This is probably due to the excessive dryness of the atmosphere, and to the haze of impalpable dust arising from the fine mud deposited by the inundation.   As the sun descends he leaves a pathway of glowing gold reflected from the smooth surface of the Nile. Any faint streaks of cloud in the west shine out as

the tenderest and most translucent bars of rose ;
a lurid reflection of the sunset lights up the
eastern sky; then half an hour after sunset a
great dome of glow arises in the west, lemon,
changing into the deepest orange, and slowly
dying away into a crimson fringe on the horizon—
the glassy mirror of the Nile gleaming like molten
metal ; and then, as the last hues of sunset fade,
the zodiacal light, a huge milky cone, shoots up
into the sky.

On moonless nights the stars shine out with a
brilliancy unknown in our misty northern latitudes.
About three in the morning the strange marvel of
the Southern Cross rises for an hour or two, the
lowest star of the four appearing through a fortunate depression in the chain of hills. When the
moon is nearly full the visitors sally out into the
temples, to enjoy in the clear, calm, and balmy air
the mystery of their dark recesses, enhanced by
the brilliant illumination of the thickly clustered
columns. It is a sight, once seen, never to be forgotten.

But the charm of Luxor does not consist mainly
in its natural beauties, though these are not to be
despised, but in its unrivalled historical interest.
There is no other site of a great ancient city which
takes you so far and so clearly back into the past.

All the greater monuments of Thebes, all the chief tombs and temples, are older than the time of Moses ; they bear in clearly readable cartouches on their sculptured walls the names of the great conquering kings of the eighteenth and nineteenth dynasties—Thothmes III., Amenhotep III., Seti I., and Rameses II.—who carried the victorious arms of Egypt to Ethiopia, Lybia, the Euphrates, and the Orontes ; the great wall-faces forming a picture-gallery of their exploits. Mere modern names on the temple-walls of Thebes are those of Shishak, who vanquished Rehoboam, and Tirhakah, the contemporary of Hezekiah. The earliest name yet found at Thebes is that of Usertasen, a king of the twelfth dynasty, who lived some forty-three centuries ago ; the latest considerable additions were made by the Ptolemies, and the record finally closes with a cartouche in which we spell out the hieroglyphic name of the Emperor Tiberius. But practically the monumental history of Thebes has ended before that of ancient Rome begins. The arches of Titus and Constantine, the mausoleum of Hadrian, Trajan's Column, the Colosseum, and the Catacombs—in short, all the great structures of pre-Christian Rome—date from a time when Thebes had begun to be forsaken, and the ruin of her temples had commenced. Even the oldest

Roman monuments, the Cloaca Maxima, the Agger, and the sub-structures of the Palatine belong to a period when the greater edifices of Thebes were hoary with the dust of centuries. When Herodotus, the father of European history, voyaged up the Nile to Thebes, at a time when the Greeks had not even heard of an obscure Italian town which bore the name of Rome, the great temples which he saw, the vocal Memnon which is the statue of Amenhotep III., and the buildings which he ascribed to a king he called Sesostris, already belonged to an antiquity as venerable as that which separates the Heptarchy and the Anglo-Saxon Kings from the reign of Queen Victoria.

Difficult as it is to realize the antiquity of these monuments, in many of which the chiselling is as sharp and the colouring as brilliant as if they had been executed only yesterday, it is still more difficult by any description to convey an impression of their vastness. The temples and tombs are scattered over a space of many square miles; single ruins cover an area of several acres; thousands of square yards of wall contain only the pictured story of a single campaign. For splendour and magnitude the group of temples at Karnak, about two miles from Luxor, forms the most magnificent ruin in the world. The temple area is surrounded by a wall of crude brick, in some places still 50 ft. in height, along the top of which you may ride for half an hour.  The great hall of the great temple measures 170 ft. by 329 ft., and the roof, single stones of which weigh 80 tons, is supported by 134 massive columns 60 ft. in height.  The forest of columns stands so thick that from no one spot is it possible to see the whole area of this stupendous hall ; and weeks may easily be spent in following the detail of the pictures which cover the outer walls of this and the adjacent temples.  We see representations of battles, sieges, sea-fights, pro-cessions of captives, offerings to the gods, massacres of prisoners, embassies from foreign lands bearing gifts and tribute, voyages of scientific exploration and their results, strange plants and animals brought from distant lands ; in short, the whole history of Egypt during the most splendid period of her greatness is recorded on the walls and pylons of the Theban temples.  And when the temples are exhausted the necropolis of Thebes still remains to be explored : itself a vast city contain-ing the dead of countless generations ; the cave-tombs penetrating deep into the heart of the mountain, with their walls painted with represen-tations of the daily life of their owners or scenes of future judgment in the Halls of Amenti.

The drawback of Thebes as a winter residence
for invalids is that the two hotels, which can
accommodate about one hundred visitors, are sadly
overcrowded, and offer no special provisions for
their comfort. The stone floors are only matted ;
the doors and windows do not close properly.
Glass is such a novelty that a broken pane can
only be replaced from Cairo, nearly five hundred
miles distant. There are no fireplaces, no bells, and
no housemaids ; and if any service is required at
night, the only means of obtaining it is to stand in
an open corridor in the cool night air, and clap
your hands till an attendant arrives. The dust-
storms are a serious discomfort, and the impalpable
dust is so fine that no precaution will exclude it
from the rooms ; while the howling of the village
dogs and the chorus of the jackals often make
sleep impossible during the best hours of the night.
But in spite of all drawbacks, many of which will
doubtless speedily be remedied, it may be affirmed
that Luxor stands unequalled among all known
winter health-resorts available for Englishmen.

# XII.

## ENGLISH AND NATIVE ADMINISTRATION.

THREE months ago, when the earlier entries were made in this Note-book, I had, by a fortunate accident, been thrown almost exclusively into the society of native gentlemen and statesmen. More recently I have had the opportunity of making the acquaintance of several able and accomplished Englishmen who occupy high positions in the Egyptian Government. It is needless to say that the Egyptian and English officials are not entirely agreed as to the wisdom of the reforms we have introduced. But if, in the first instance, I had fallen into the English society of Cairo, it would have been more difficult to have reported, without bias, the conversation of the native Pashas, and I am not sure that they would have spoken to me so freely as they did. My former notes represent —faithfully, as I believe—the tone of intelligent native opinion, as to which it is most desirable that we should be informed, and which has not, so far as I know, been adequately set forth in the English press. It is less needful to state the views of the English officials, as they have been ably and amply reproduced in the Egyptian correspondence of the *Times*. I will therefore only refer to matters as to which the statements of my native informants require to be supplemented or corrected.

The Egyptians, as I have already said, think that some of our "reforms" were hasty or inexpedient. The English, on the other hand, think we have not gone far enough, and point to the defective administration of justice, which has hitherto been left in the hands of native administrators, and to the improvement in the material condition of the people, which, they contend, is due to the changes we have introduced. It cannot be denied that the signs of increasing prosperity are everywhere manifest, and this is the case in the provinces even more than in the capital. Either the people are growing more wealthy, or a feeling of security, due mainly to the English occupation, makes them more ready to exhibit their wealth, or to employ hoarded treasures in the erection of new houses. The burden of indebtedness to the Greek usurers, who have established themselves in most of the small towns and larger villages, is growing less ;

indeed, I was told on high authority that it is estimated that during the last six years the indebtedness of the peasantry has diminished from about six millions sterling to a little more than two millions. This result seems largely due to reforms in the mode in which the taxes are collected. Illegal exactions are now difficult. The fellah knows exactly how much he will have to pay; and he is no longer liable to be called upon to produce his rent, his taxes, or his irrigation rate several months in advance, long before his harvest is ready for the market—an extortion which frequently made it needful for him to mortgage his growing crops to the village usurer at a ruinous rate of interest.

Another source of increasing wealth must be set down to the excellent administration of the Public Works Department by Sir Colin Scott Moncrieff and the able staff of assistant engineers he has gathered round him. The prosperity of Egypt depends mainly on the facilities for irrigation, and I find everywhere that new canals are being dug, or the old ones deepened and improved. During the last five years, I was told, something like 2,000,000 acres have been added to the productive area of Egypt; and the work still goes on. Walking one day with an engineer in the

Irrigation Department along the banks of one of the subsidiary canals in Upper Egypt, I ventured to ask him some questions about its cost and its commercial value. This canal, he said, is ten miles long and cost about £120 a mile to dig. Its construction has made it possible to obtain a second, or even a third crop from about 5000 acres; the annual letting value of which has been increased by a sum of between sixty and seventy shillings an acre. Such a work would, therefore, return more than cent. per cent. per annum on its prime cost. He went on to speak of another great work on which he is engaged, the Nubarieh Canal in the extreme west of the Delta, which, at an estimated cost of £70,000, will make it possible to irrigate and bring into cultivation 64,000 acres of land which are now waste. He has also made an estimate for a new canal in the Fayoom, which will, it is computed, add between £6 and £7 to the selling value of each acre benefited, at an outlay of about eighteen shillings an acre. He finally referred me to his report for 1886, the last published, from which I find that in one case a capital expenditure of £5,476 has rendered needless an annual charge of at least £7,200; in another case the outlay of £1887 has resulted in a saving of £1500 a year;

while 400 acres, reclaimed at a total cost of £30, had been sold for £4000. These, of course, are exceptional instances, and there are not many works of so profitable a character still remaining to be executed.

The benefits conferred on Egypt by English management are chiefly apparent in the two Departments of Finance and Public Works; both under able chiefs, who, being comparatively unfettered by foreign or native interference, have had a free hand. In striking contrast with the Department of Public Works is the administration of the railways, which are under a sort of international control. Three directors—an Egyptian, a Frenchman, and an Englishman, none of whom have any special knowledge of railway administration—are employed at high salaries in doing, or rather in leaving undone, work which would not overtax the powers of the manager of one of the smaller English lines. International jealousies have, however, to be satisfied ; and the result is that the work is badly done, the trains are few, slow, and unpunctual, the fares high, the carriages dirty, the charges for luggage extortionate, and the lavatory arrangements execrable. The Daira and the Domains, also under international control, are said to be greatly mis-

managed. There is an annual deficit on these
estates of about a quarter of a million, which has
to be made good out of the general revenue. One
Pasha told me that the sugar lands were let by
auction—a Western arrangement unsuited to the
East—and fetched sums greatly under their real
value. The auction, he said (and he had good
opportunities of knowing), usually resulted in a
knock-out. The chief men of the district met
and agreed among themselves as to what lands
would suit them, and what price they should offer.
" But suppose," I said, " some independent person
were to bid and run the land up to a fair price,
what would happen ? " " Nothing," was the reply,
"could be more simple. The interloper would be
accused of some crime—murder possibly, or more
probably of forgery—and by false accusation
would be thrown into prison till he consented to
give up the land." "What remedy," I said,
"would you suggest ? " "Get rid of all the State
lands as soon as purchasers can be found, and
meanwhile abolish the present costly staff of
managers. The letting of the land might be
entrusted to the Mudirs, who know the people
and would obtain a better price by private tender
and at less cost for management. Two-thirds of
the clerks might be dispensed with, and the rest

should be turned over to other departments in which the offices are undermanned. In some provinces the present staff of clerks cannot get through the work, and a large number of unpaid supernumeraries are employed who necessarily live by bribes. In one provincial office," said my informant, "I found thirty clerks drawing no salaries." "How do they live, then?" "Say a process has to be served, the head clerk goes to one of the unpaid subordinates, and says, 'You have not had a job for some time. You may serve this process.' The clerk goes, receives a bribe, and reports that he has been unable to find the person required. The same operation is repeated at intervals again and again for months. At last the case is heard, and judgment is ultimately given ; but is not executed till after similar delays."

I have heard many stories tending to show the unsatisfactory administration of the Department of Justice, which has hitherto been left almost entirely under native control. The mixed tribunals, I was told, were often the source of frightful injustice, and it was very difficult for a native to obtain redress against a clever rogue under foreign protection. If he found the case going against him, he would either change his allegiance or transfer the cause of action to the subject of some other Power; in either of which cases the whole action would have to be begun again in another court. "So long as the Capitulations are in force," said a native judge, "real justice is impossible in Egypt. There is one thing," he added, "by which you English might have earned our everlasting gratitude. When the French took Tunis they abolished the Capitulations, and good government at once became possible. In like manner, when you first occupied Egypt you might with a high hand have declared that the Capitulations were needless, and no Power would have ventured to interfere. But you did not know your own minds, or you did not realize how impossible it would be for you to evacuate the country; and you foolishly talked about going away in six months. You have only yourselves to thank for the difficulties which now embarrass you."

The most intelligent of all the Mudirs to whom I had letters of introduction, said very nearly the same thing. Of all the reforms needed in Egypt, he said, the most necessary is the abolition of the Capitulations. How would you get on in England, he added, if seventeen European Powers possessed treaty rights which allowed them to interfere with

H

the administration of justice, or enabled any one
of them to veto some urgent domestic reform?

But even when the cause lies between two
natives, difficulties occur which seem incredible to
Western minds.  A Pasha told me the following
curious story, which sounds like an incident out
of the "Arabian Nights."  A short time ago, he
said, I had to investigate a case in which Ahmed's
camel was accused of trespassing on Suleiman's
land, and doing damage to the crops.  The testimony produced was clear and overwhelming.
But not long afterwards I had occasion to visit
the village where the parties lived, and I thought
I would go and have a look at the land.  I found,
to my surprise, that no one was able to point it
out.  On further inquiry I discovered that Ahmed
possessed no camel, and that Suleiman had got
no land.  I asked Suleiman to tell me confidentially why he had brought such a ridiculous suit.
Then it appeared that the real cause of quarrel
was that Ahmed's slave had looked over the wall
of Suleiman's harem, and the inmates had considered themselves insulted.  As, owing to Moslem
etiquette, the real witnesses could not be brought
into open court, both parties had agreed to try
a false issue by means of suborned testimony.  So
the fictitious camel stood for the slave, and the

fictitious land for the harem. Such are the "affairs of Egypt."

I heard another characteristic story, which shows how greatly the native tribunals are in need of reform. A man named Mahomet, a resident at Khartoum, shortly before the siege, for greater security, entrusted his whole fortune, amounting to £1600, to his friend, the Mamur of a large town in Upper Egypt, and promised him £200 for his trouble. When Khartoum fell, the Mamur put on mourning for his friend, who, he gave out, had gone to the mercy of Allah. He kept the money, on the ground that it had lapsed to him as the cousin and dear friend of the deceased. After a while, however, Mahomet turned up and demanded the restitution of his money. The Mamur denounced him as an impostor, declaring that he had never seen him before in his life. Mahomet sent for his wife to testify to his identity; whereupon the Mamur generously offered, as a special mark of regard for his deceased friend, to marry her, as on his theory she was now a widow. The case was taken before the local judge, who informed the Mamur that unless he gave £500 as backsheesh he would have to disgorge the whole sum. The Mamur considered the proposal extortionate, and the case went up on appeal to Cairo; where the Mamur expended £1100 in squaring the officials all round. The balance he succeeded in keeping for himself, while poor Mahomet lost his fortune and was condemned in costs. What became of the wife I did not hear.

The native president of one of the local tribunals told me some heart-breaking stories of the hardships to which the people have to submit. A peasant was summoned as a witness in some unimportant case. The testimony he had to give was of a trivial nature, and the matter was no concern of his. The witness lived in a village two days' journey from the town where the cause was to be tried. The poor man was blind, and it was needful for his wife to come with him to lead him by the hand. She had two children who could not be left behind, one of them being a babe in arms. They were very poor, and had to walk the whole distance; and, on their arrival, had to sleep in the street, as they could not pay for a lodging. The case was not reached, and they were told to go away and come again in a week. The same thing happened five or six times. The weather was inclement, and both the children died from hunger and exposure. My informant, with tears in his eyes and his voice broken with emotion, told me how at last the desperate mother caught hold of his robe as he left the tribunal, saying, "You, sir, are the president of this tribunal. See what we have suffered ; put an end to this misery and injustice." My friend, much moved, took the next train to Cairo, and told the story to the Pasha responsible for the administration of justice, who, however, refused to do anything to remedy the cruelty or to prevent such things happening in future. My friend, a most humane man, was so indignant that he resigned his post.

Obviously I am not in a position personally to guarantee the accuracy of any of the foregoing stories. I only profess to narrate them as they were told me by gentlemen of position, whose good faith I have no reason to distrust.

By the abolition of the kourbash and the corvée, and by other similar reforms, we have made native administration on the old lines impossible, while the Department of Justice has hardly yet been touched. To leave Egypt in chaos, with our reforms half completed, would be a crime. Obviously the only righteous course is to go on, and bestow on Egypt the same good government we have given to India. In the opinion of those who seem to be the best informed—Englishmen, as well as natives—this should be done as far as possible by native agency; but the agents will have to be trained. The Oriental vices of bribery and falsehood must be rooted out. The best men obtainable should be selected for the important office of Mudir. They should not be fettered and humiliated by too much European supervision; they should receive salaries which will make it worth their while to refuse bribes, and summary dismissal should follow on any proved case of oppression or extortion. Above all, it should be remembered that we cannot make Egyptians into Englishmen, or govern them on principles applicable to England. The form of government should be Oriental; it must, in short, be a despotism of some kind, tempered by European control ; but the despots should be wise, beneficent, and honest. As for local self-government, carried on by elective talking machinery, even Egyptian Radicals did not advocate it.

# XIII.

## MAHOMMEDANS ON MAHOMMEDANISM.

I WENT to Egypt, the heart of Islam, mainly that I might study on the spot the practical working of the vast code of morals, devotion, and religion which is contained in the Koran ; and, if possible, ascertain for myself the actual beliefs of educated Moslems. In this attempt I met with no obstacles, as it was known that I was not attempting to make prose-lytes. It is true that there is a feeling of soreness among Mahommedans because they believe that they have been cruelly libelled and misunderstood by Christians. They complain that though they regard us as brother-believers and accept our Scriptures, they are nevertheless denounced as infidels. "Why," I have been asked, "should an eternal coldness reign in your hearts ?"

I confess I was surprised at the willingness of Mahommedans to talk freely on the subject of their beliefs, and at their readiness in admitting shortcomings in matters of conduct. "We do not shrink from inquiry," said a learned Moslem, who, like many others, was familiar with the Bible as well as with the Koran. "We welcome the fullest discussion ; it can only serve to bring out the truth. Let us talk the matter over, and you will see in how many things we agree and in how few we differ. It ought not to be difficult to come to an understanding. Doubtless there are things which we shall have to give up. We have added many things " (he meant the traditions and the commentaries) " to the purity of our revealed scriptures ; but you have done the same. Our religion, like yours, has been corrupted. Many of our popular beliefs and practices" (he named some of them) " have no more support from the Koran than the image-worship and Mariolatry of Christians have in the New Testament. If we return to the pure teaching of Mahommed and you return to the pure teaching of Jesus Christ and His Apostles, we shall find few points of difference to divide us. Your primitive Christianity we accept ; but we consider that as early as the time of Constantine the teaching of the Apostolic age had become overlaid with superstitions which should be rejected. The time will come," he added, " when both Christians and Moslems will cast aside these corruptions, and there will be one pure faith which all will be able to accept."

Having recently seen something of the Mariolatry and iconolatry of the Copts, from whom the Egyptian Moslems chiefly gather their notions of Christianity, I thought that my friend was understating his case, and felt that an educated Englishman might have almost as much in common with an intelligent Moslem as with an illiterate Copt. It would be unreasonable to expect Mahommedans, at our mere bidding, to discard doctrines and forms of devotion in which they have been brought up, and to embrace the narrow dogmas of missionaries who are endeavouring to convert them to some one of the discordant forms of Romanist or Protestant belief. They accept the New Testament; but, like the Protestant sects, they claim the right of putting their own interpretation on it. They repudiate altogether such modern formularies as the Thirty-Nine Articles, the Westminster Confession, or the Tridentine decrees.

Every Moslem believes devoutly in a personal God, in an overruling Providence, in the mission and miracles of Christ, whom they designate as the Messiah, in the duty of prayer, in the immortality of the soul, in a future state of rewards and punishments, and in the inspiration of the Bible.

The Mahommedans are most devout; and some of their prayers are beautiful in the extreme, without a word to which the most fastidious could object, and in which it would be less difficult for many of us to join than in some extemporaneous Protestant addresses to the Deity or in certain Romanist invocations of the " Queen of Heaven " —*spes unica peccatorum.* Take, for instance, the Fatha—a prayer which all Moslems offer twice daily, morning and evening—

> " Praise be to God, Master of the Universe,
> The Merciful, the Compassionate,
> Lord of the Day of Judgment.
> Thee only do we worship,
> To Thee do we cry for help.
> Guide us in the right way ;
> In the way of those whom Thou hast loaded with Thy blessings,
> Not in the way of those who have encountered Thy wrath, or who
> have gone astray."

Another prayer, called the Prayer of David, runs thus—

> " O Lord, grant to me the love of Thee ; grant that I may love those who love Thee ; grant that I may do the deeds that may win Thy love ; make Thy love to be dearer to me than myself or my family, dearer than wealth, dearer even than cool water."

Or take this devout prayer—

> " O God ! grant us Thy help, Thy pity, and Thy guidance in the right way. We believe in Thee, we turn to Thee for aid, we put our trust in Thee, we acknowledge Thee to be source of all good. We give Thee thanks, we do not fail to recognize Thy goodness, we

humble ourselves before Thee, and we walk not with such as are disobedient to Thy will. Thee, O God, do we adore ; before Thee we bend our knees, to Thee we offer our prayers and praises. We implore Thy mercy and we dread Thy wrath, which those who do evil have deserved."

This last prayer will bear comparison, not altogether to the disadvantage of the Mahommedans, with some Christian devotions, such as the following invocation to the Virgin Mary, to every repetition of which the Pope, in 1840, attached an Indulgence of one hundred years : "O immaculate Queen of Heaven and of the Angels, I adore Thee ! It is Thou who hast delivered me from hell. It is to Thee that I look for all my salvation !" Or this, which is taken from the Office of the B.V.M. : "In Thee do we trust, on Thee we place our hope. Do Thou defend us to all eternity." Can we wonder that Mahommedans prefer their own prayers to those of the Romanist missionaries who are endeavouring to convert them ? On the other hand, it would not be difficult to compile, from Mahommedan formularies, a book of devotion which, if its origin were unknown, might be welcomed in Christian lands.

It is curious to note how almost every doctrine of Islam has been held by some Christian sect or by some Christian writer. Thus all Moslems would unreservedly accept the definition of God

contained in the Westminster Confession. Their
opinions as to Predestination and the Divine
Sovereignty are those of Calvin ; their doctrine as
to the brotherhood of believers is that of the
Wesleyans. As to the sacraments and the priest-
hood, they agree with the Quakers and Mr. Bright ;
as to the Trinity, with the Unitarians and Mr.
Chamberlain ; and as to tithes, with Lord Selborne
and Mr. Beresford-Hope. Their doctrine of inspiration is almost precisely that of the Dean of
Chichester ; their views as to the nature of future
punishment are those of Dr. Pusey, while as to
its duration they incline to the opinions of Arch-
deacon Farrar ; and they would accept more
readily than some of us Dr. Cumming's opinions
concerning the second Advent, or Canon Body's
belief as to the terrestrial functions discharged by
angels. They hold, with the soundest Anglican
divines, that the object of prayer is not to conform
God's will to ours, but ours to His. Far more
reverent than the Salvation Army, their missionaries, like those of General Booth, preach one
chief doctrine, salvation by faith, and insist on one
chief practice, abstinence from alcohol. There is
hardly a single doctrine of Islam that has not been
advocated by some whom we recognize as Christians, while no Moslems hold legends or superstitions

so gross as those which are entertained by the peasantry of Southern Italy.

On various points as to which they differ from us they appeal to the Bible to justify their belief and practices. Thus they defend the permission of polygamy and concubinage in the Koran by the examples of David, Solomon, Jacob, and Abraham, whom they reverence as "prophets;" while as for the reproach of slavery they contend, like the American slave-owners in recent times, that it is not prohibited even in the New Testament— Philemon having been the owner of a runaway slave, who was sent back by the Apostle Paul, who commands slaves to be obedient to their masters. But though they hold that polygamy, concubinage, and slavery are not expressly forbidden in the Koran any more than in the Old Testament, many of them are decidedly of opinion that they are no longer expedient, and that the time has arrived when they should be prohibited or given up as anachronisms. "They are very great evils," said more than one Mahommedan, and the general opinion seems to be that the force of public opinion will soon abolish them for ever.

The "holy wars," to which Islam owed some of its earlier triumphs, are defended by the example of the conquest of Canaan by the Israelites; and we are asked whether the Caliphs were not more merciful than Joshua, than Samuel when he enjoined the slaughter of Agag and the Amalekites, or than Elijah, who put to death the four hundred and fifty priests of Baal. And if it be urged that these are events in Jewish and not in Christian history, they reply that Christian history is not unstained by religious wars or free from the reproach that it has been propagated by the sword. It would be difficult to find a parallel in Moslem history to Justinian's extermination of the Montanists, or to his baptism by force of seventy thousand pagans in Asia Minor ; or, coming down to later times, Islam cannot be reproached with atrocities so horrible as the crusade of Innocent III. against the Albigenses, the massacre of St. Bartholomew, Charlemagne's war of extermination against the pagan Saxons, the expulsion of the Moors and Moriscoes from Spain, or the mediæval persecutions of the Jews ; while the slaughter of ten thousand Moslems after the capture of Antioch by the Crusaders, or the massacre of seventy thousand Moslems when Jerusalem was taken by Godfrey of Bouillon, may be contrasted with the mercy shown by Omar at the first Moslem capture of Jerusalem, or by Saladin when it was recovered from the Crusaders.

The Mahommedans urge—and I think with truth —that their annals are less bloodstained than the annals of the Christians ; and if it be said that the Crusades are ancient history, so also, they plead, are the crescentades.  But these questions, which have hitherto been judiciously evaded by Canon Malcolm MacColl, may be left to him to deal with in the next article he writes on " Islam and Civilization " in the *Contemporary.*  I confess I should much like to be present at a discussion between that able controversialist and some of my Mahommedan friends—not less able, and possibly not less learned.  " Honours divided," would, I expect, be the decision of the umpire.

Another accusation is that Islam is sterile and unprogressive.  But the same may be said of other Oriental religions.  It is a question of race and climate rather than of creed.  The Coptic Church is even more immobile than Islam.  The service-books, the order of the worship, and the arrangements of the churches are the same as they were in the third century ; nothing has been changed. I think there are fewer signs of progress among the Copts than among the Moslems.  The same might be said of Hindoos, Buddhists, and Con-fucians.  Asiatics are free from our restlessness. But of this Canon MacColl takes no account ; he contrasts Western energy with Oriental inertness, and attributes the whole difference to religion. This he explains by the assumption that for Mahommedans "any progress beyond the Koran is not only superfluous but impious in addition." This may be the opinion of Canon MacColl, but it is not the opinion of Mahommedans themselves. They freely admit that, like other Orientals, they are behindhand in their knowledge of modern science; but they are proud of the scientific acquirements of the brilliant period of Arab history, and an ardent desire for progress and education is not uncommon. I have already mentioned the remarkable fact that the Sheikh-el-Azhar, who occupies much the same position as the Vice-Chancellor of an English university, recently applied to the Egyptian Minister of Education to provide instruction in secular science for twelve hundred of his theological students. A Mahommedan, who had been a professor in one of the Government colleges, told me that he had inserted a paragraph in one of the vernacular newspapers offering to lecture on science to a few of the El Azhar students, and that in one week he received no fewer than sixteen hundred applications for admission to the class. The most useful teaching for such students would be a knowledge of history, but the difficulty is that there are no suitable text-books treating both religions in an appreciative spirit. I asked a student at El Azhar whether he had read any history. "Yes," he said, "I have got one book; but I do not like it." "Why?" "Because it says that Mahommed was an impostor." The book proved to be a work by "Peter Parley," given him by an American missionary. No wonder he did not like it. Should we like it if Mahommedan missionaries were to distribute among the students at our theological colleges books describing the Founder of Christianity as an impostor?

It is not by such means that Mahommedans can be won over, and I am not surprised at the failure to convert them. I am informed that in Cairo the conversions from Christianity to Islam are about twice as numerous as the conversions from Islam to Christianity. A gentleman who for two years was Lieutenant-Governor of Cairo, said that during that time there were five or six conversions of Copts or Syrians to Islam, and only two or three of Moslems to Christianity. No Jew ever embraces Islam. Conversions, I was told, are not encouraged, as the motives of the convert are usually open to suspicion. An intending convert is sent to his priest to be examined as to his reasons for changing his religion. If he returns with a proper certificate, he has to appear before a judge, and the change of religion is recognized. In most instances, I hear, there is a woman in the case. A Moslem woman may not marry a Christian, but a Christian woman can marry a Moslem, and is protected in the exercise of her religion; but the children of such marriages have to be brought up as Moslems.

# XIV.

## THE BASES OF MAHOMMEDAN BELIEF.

AN educated Mahommedan, if asked why he does not become a Christian, may not improbably reply that, according to his own interpretation of the New Testament, he is one already. Thus, in a letter, received recently from one of my friends, he styles himself "a Muslim and a Christian at the same time." Though a most pious and sincere Mahommedan, he claims to be one of those "who profess and call themselves Christians," for whom we pray every Sunday that "they may be led into the way of truth." How far the profession of Islam is inconsistent with such a profession of Christianity it may be well to inquire.

Mahommedans themselves consider that their recognition of the authority of the Koran does not bar them from recognizing also the authority of the Bible ; or rather, as they would put it, they receive the Bible on the authority of the Koran.

They hold the co-ordinate authority of the Bible and the Koran as revealed and inspired books. They affirm that the Koran does not contradict the Bible, but supplements it. The Koran itself expressly states that "it is a clearing up of the Scriptures, confirming and explaining them." Mahommedans hold in especial esteem the Psalms, the Pentateuch, and the Gospels. Such of the books of the Bible as were written by any of those whom they style "Prophets," they hold to be infallible, and to contain no errors of fact or doctrine. "Do you," I once asked, "accept the writings of Paul the Apostle?" "Undoubtedly," was the reply; "we reckon him among the Prophets, and he was therefore inspired." Every word uttered by Jesus the Messiah they consider to be absolutely and infallibly true; but they say that, since His discourses were not written down for many years after they were uttered, it is possible that the Gospels, as we have them, may contain errors of transmission, some of which they hold are corrected in the Koran. They look at the Jewish and Christian faiths as revealed religions, preparatory to Islam, which was the final revelation.

They are more tolerant than we are, as they do not refuse to regard us as brother believers.

"Whom," I once asked, "do you consider to be Moslems?" A Moslem, I was told, is one who is resigned to God's will and strives after righteousness ; a Mahommedan is one who recognizes the mission of Mahommed ; but the usual name we give to Jews and Christians is *Mouminim*, which means "believers," since they have a written revelation, and are therefore "people of a book." But we consider that the belief of the Mouminim is defective rather than erroneous ; since we hold that Islam was the latest revelation, perfecting the Christian revelation, just as Christianity supplemented the revelation given to the Jews. Mahommed may be considered as a reformer of Christianity ; like Luther, he denounced certain superstitions that had grown up—such as monastic celibacy, the worship of images, of the crucifix, and of the Virgin Mary. The Koran says that God gave the Gospel to Jesus to proclaim, and that He put kindness and compassion into the hearts of those who followed Him ; but "as for the monastic life, they invented it themselves." The Prophet Paul himself says that in the latter times some shall depart from the faith, speaking lies and forbidding to marry. "In the time of Mahommed," said one of my friends, "Christianity had become corrupt, as many of your own writers admit; and it was these corruptions that it was Mahommed's mission to reform. We reject the corruptions of Christianity; but there is nothing in your sacred books that we do not accept, though we may differ with you as to the text or the interpretation, just as Christian sects differ among themselves. But we claim to have a final revelation, predicted by your own prophets; just as the coming of the Messiah was foretold to the Jews, who nevertheless blindly rejected Him, as you reject Mahommed."

I gather that Mahommedans would accept without reserve the arguments of such a book as Paley's "Evidences" as conclusive of the divine origin of Christianity; but they consider that, to a great extent, the same arguments are valid in favour of the claims of Islam. Thus they appeal, as "evidences" of its truth, to the marvellous rapidity of its early diffusion, and to the manifest sincerity of the disciples of Mahommed, as proved by their constancy under persecution and martyrdom. They appeal also to the intrinsic beauty of the precepts of the Koran, to their wonderful adaptation to the religious needs of human nature, and to the elevating and ennobling influence they have exercised over the minds and conduct of its professors, giving them dignity, serenity, and resignation under trial and misfortune. Is it credible, they say, that a simple and unlearned man like Mahommed could have enunciated the pure and lofty truths contained in the Koran without divine guidance ?

As to the question of miracles, while accepting without hesitation those recorded in the Bible, Mahommedans affirm that the absence of the miraculous element in Islám is only a proof of its truth. If Mahommed had been a deceiver, he could easily, they say, have imposed on his disciples by pretended miracles. They add that Jesus only resorted to them because of the stubborn unbelief of the Jews, constantly reproaching them for requiring signs and wonders ; while if He had steadfastly refused to perform them, one difficulty in the way of the reception of His religion would have been removed, since the miraculous element in Christianity is now becoming a difficulty rather than a help to Christian apologists. That Mahommed refused to appeal to miracles, real or pretended, but relied for his credentials exclusively on the internal evidence of his teaching, is therefore, they urge, no difficulty, but rather the reverse.

Mahommedans, however, rely confidently on the argument from prophecy. They hold that the mission of Mahommed was foretold as clearly and as constantly as that of the Messiah, and they quote numerous passages from the Old and the New Testaments in support of this belief. On the other hand, certain prophecies which writers in the *Record* and the *Rock* refer to Islam, Mahommedans apply with equal confidence to the crusades. Thus the "little horn" of Daniel, as well as the king of the locusts coming up out of the bottomless pit, which are identified by Christian commentators with Mahommed, they refer to Godfrey of Bouillon; who is appropriately called Abaddon, the destroyer, since he massacred seventy thousand Moslems at the capture of the Holy City. What can be plainer, they say, than the reference to the horses and iron breastplates of his knights?

It may be worth while to give another specimen of their arguments. One of my friends called my particular attention to the final verses of the book of Daniel. . Dating the cessation of the daily sacrifice from the erection of heathen altars in the temple by Manasseh, and identifying the graven idol which he set up in the holy place with the abomination which maketh desolation (the desolation being the Assyrian capture of Jerusalem which forthwith ensued) the two periods of 1290 and 1335 years mentioned by Daniel bring us, the first to the Hegira as "the time of the end," and the second to the Caliphate of Moawiya, when, Persia, Syria, Egypt, and Northern Africa having been subdued, the death of Ali and the abdication of Hassan brought the great schism to an end, and the Moslems had rest from internal and external conflict, and "stood in their lot at the end of the days." This interpretation, though perhaps not less plausible than some of those that have been advanced, is open to such obvious objections, that it need not be seriously discussed ; but the point really worthy of note is the confidence with which Mahommedans appeal to Jewish and Christian prophecy in support of the claims of their religion.

One of the commonest reproaches thrown in the teeth of Mahommedans is that they believe in a material, sensual Paradise, provided with black-eyed houris for the delectation of the faithful. Canon MacColl, for instance, thinks "we shall all agree" in the opinion, which he quotes from another writer, that the Mahommedan notion of a future life is "the plenary enjoyment of an ever-lasting brothel." There are few things which ardent controversialists are unable to believe of those who differ from them ; but I am entitled to say that educated Mahommedans, who ought to know best what they really believe, would repudiate such a description with horror and indignation. They claim to interpret the Koran not by isolated texts but by its general scope. In the Song of Solomon, they say, there are passages which, if interpreted literally, are more sensuous than any in the Koran ; but the headings in the Authorized Version explain them as descriptive of " the mutual love of Christ and His Church." Even as to a material Paradise, the Koran hardly falls short of the description of the New Jerusalem in the Book of Revelation, with its crystal sea, its gates of pearl, its streets of gold, and its walls of precious stones. There is nothing in their worship more open to misconstruction than the favourite paraphrase sung with such unction in our churches, describing " Jerusalem the golden, with milk and honey blest." Moslems might allege that the description of " the shouts of them that triumph, the songs of them that feast " reproduces, as elements of the Christian Paradise, the noisy revelry, the gluttony and drunkenness, and the swaggering songs which scandalize the staid and sober Moslems when the bibulous festivities of Western nations take place in Cairo. They say that in the Book of Revelation there is no hint that the description of the New Jerusalem is figurative, but that we are expressly told "these sayings are faithful and true," whereas the Koran itself enjoins them to interpret its account of Paradise as figurative. They urge that, while the Revelation is the final book in the Bible, the later Suras in the Koran show a more spiritual conception of the future life than the earlier ones. And they refer to a late Sura (III. 5) in which Mahommed says that in the Koran "some things are of themselves clear to understand and others are figurative." That this applies especially to the descriptions of Paradise in the Koran is supported by the Traditions; which tell us that Mahommed, talking with his friends of the blessedness of the future life, said that "the greatest blessedness of all will be to see the Lord's glory night and morning, a felicity which will surpass all the pleasures of the body as the ocean surpasses a drop of sweat." On another occasion he said, "The good will enjoy the beatific vision of God;" and again, almost in the words of St. Paul, he stated, "God hath prepared for His good people what no eye hath seen or ear heard, nor hath it entered into the heart of any one."

The Mahommedans therefore allege that they have more justification for interpreting figuratively the description of Paradise in the Koran than we have for interpreting figuratively certain passages in the Song of Solomon or the Revelation. It is, I think, manifestly unfair to deny them a principle of exegesis which we claim to use ourselves in the interpretation of the Bible. In any case we shall certainly not convert them by insisting upon interpretations of the Koran which they themselves disclaim. They would not succeed in converting us by asserting that all Christians deify the Virgin Mary. The polemic methods of hostile controversy are not calculated to produce conviction, but rather the reverse. It is wiser to minimise, rather than to accentuate, points of difference. By leading our antagonists to believe that we are intolerant, unreasonable, and unjust, we are not likely to secure a favourable consideration for our arguments.

## XV

## PROSPECTS OF A MOSLEM REFORMATION.

AT the last Church Congress I said that Islam might be regarded as a semi-Christian, rather than an anti-Christian faith, and that since Moslems recognize the New Testament as one of their sacred books, and receive its teaching as inspired, we should endeavour, instead of denouncing them as infidels, to develop those elements of Christian teaching which they accept. For venturing to say these things I have been reviled by the "religious" press, preached against by Bishops, denounced as a traitor from missionary platforms, and have alienated many valued friends. I have been informed on anonymous post-cards that I "must be an awful man," and have been compared in the columns of the *Guardian* to Goliath "defying the armies of the living God."

Leaving England in the midst of this wintry tempest of Protestant fanaticism, I landed on the calm and sunny shores of Egypt. The difference in the religious temper of the two lands was as marked as the difference in the climate. I found more of the spirit of religious tolerance and of true Christian charity in the East than in the West. The echoes of the stormy controversy, with its wild abuse of Islam and all its works, were still reverberating in the vernacular journals of Cairo, Constantinople, Beyrout, and Teheran; but instead of producing, as in England, explosions of fierce intolerance, I found a yearning for brotherly concord with Christians, and a desire for a reformation which might bring Islam into a closer approach to Christianity, so that, as one of my Mahommedan friends expresses it, there might be "a mutual embrace of affection, the touching of hands in friendship, and the disappearance of the swords of war."

This is the case not only in Egypt, but in Syria, Turkey, Persia, India, and China. In all these countries enlightened Mahommedans are beginning to question the finality of their old beliefs, and to ask whether the New Testament, of which they express their entire acceptance, may not contain teaching which they have misunderstood or overlooked. This ferment manifests itself in a wish for a more brotherly relationship with Christians, and a desire to find some common

ground of external fellowship. What I said at
Wolverhampton as to the acceptance of the
teaching of the New Testament by Moslems has,
as one of them writes to me, "been translated
into various Mahommedan languages in all
Mahommedan countries." How enthusiastically
this offer of the olive-branch has been acclaimed
by Moslems I can only prove by quoting, at the
risk of a charge of egotism, from some of the
letters I have received. A Persian Soufi, who
possesses great influence at Tehcran, and who is
the son of a celebrated Mahommedan saint,
"invokes the blessing of the Ineffable Unity on
my luminous Existence," and sends me his
"thousandfold thanks" for the expression of
opinions with which he substantially agrees. He
affirms that there is "no essential contradiction
whatever" between the opinions of enlightened
persons of both religions, and hopes that "the
trammels of custom may be burst, and Christians
and Moslems be brought together in mutual
meeting."

Another Persian, residing in Syria, who by
frequent quotations shows that he is a diligent
student of the New Testament, writes :—"I con-
gratulate you on the favourable impression which
your illustrious speech has made on the Mahom-

medans in this country, all of whom seem to be thunderstruck by the joyful news." He narrates his own efforts to establish a mutual good understanding between Moslems and Christians, believing that "the way to be called sons of God is by becoming peacemakers." Though now, he says, too old to hope to see the fulfilment of such blessed ideas of brotherhood and peace, he is able to say, with Simeon, "Lord, now lettest Thou Thy servant depart in peace; for mine eyes have seen Thy salvation." He hopes "some young, enthusiastic Mahommedans" may receive a proper training, and " be sent forth to the East as missionaries of union to establish schools and proclaim peace around. The Lord be with you. It rests with you and your God-loving party, who make mention of the Lord, not to keep silence."

Moslems are already offering themselves as missionaries of this gospel of peace and goodwill. A young Turkish Bey proposes to come to England "to be better instructed in the religion of the Messiah," that he may return to the East as a teacher. "Most Mohammedans," he says, "have long ago been desirous of religious concord with Christians." He thinks the Bible and the Koran "jointly establish the true path, and, if all were to act in accordance with the precepts of their own scriptures, there would be little difference except in the name of the obligation. In the name of God, let us begin together this work for the concord of religions."

A pious and learned Sheikh, educated at the Moslem University of El Azhar, and greatly esteemed as an authority on religious questions, thanks me for "clothing in a beautiful garb the words of equity," and for endeavouring to dispel the "falsifications" which prevail as to the real doctrines of Islam. He goes on to say, "The light of truth shines from thy discourse. The darkness of ignorance is dispelled, and the dawning of light is arising to the two great religions." He refers to "the acceptance of the religion of the Messiah in Islam," and affirms that the Koran and the Bible "agree with one another, and are a righteousness to all in their study. Therefore let the children of the two religions meet on the only road that is true, and become perfect in the light of God. The perfecting of the work would be the sending out of men who agree with thee, to establish schools in the East, and impress this revered way on the pure minds of the children. As for me, I am ready to assist thee as regards an approach between the two religions. And if thou hast other sayings, we

K

desire that thou wouldest send them, that we may spread them among the people of the East, who are Arabs and Turks and others. Now let there be peace on all who follow the true guidance." The beautiful and touching letter from which the foregoing extracts are taken breathes, I think, the spirit of true Christian charity, and is valuable as showing the earnest longing of pious Moslems for religious concord with Christians, and their friendly feelings towards those by whom they think they have been so grievously misunderstood. The "united Church" which one of my enthusiastic correspondents desires to establish, would apparently add to the teaching of the Sermon on the Mount the Koranic prohibitions of alcohol, gambling, and cruelty to animals— precepts essentially needed in the East. Instruction out of the New Testament might be given as freely in the proposed schools as in our English Board schools, since a Mahommedan boy on leaving school makes a solemn "Covenant with the Creator," in which he professes his faith in the Bible as well as in the Koran.

The spirit which pervades the letters from which I have quoted prevails among Mahommedans with whom I have recently conversed. In Cairo I encountered no vestige of intolerance or fanaticism,

but have been met with the utmost cordiality, and
with a generous appreciation of my efforts to
promote mutual good-feeling, and I have found
a singular readiness to discuss in a friendly spirit
the differences between the two religions, and
the reforms which might be needful to bring
Islam into harmony with Western modes of
thought.

A proof of the open-mindedness of Mahommedans, and of the way in which they welcome
the prospect of a better understanding between
Christians and themselves, was afforded by the
enthusiasm with which I was received by some of
the students at the theological university of El Azhar,
which possesses vast endowments for teaching the
doctrines of Islam, and where eight thousand
students from every quarter of the Mahommedan
world are being trained as the future teachers of
150 millions of Mahommedans. I wish that Canon
MacColl, who thinks "it is no exaggeration to say
that the teaching in Mahommedan schools is for
the most part a mixture of fanaticism, intolerance,
and vice," could have accompanied me on a visit
to El Azhar, the greatest of all Moslem schools.
There is zeal if you will, and there is more apparent
reverence and devoutness than among students
designed for the Christian ministry at Oxford or

Cambridge. I have never witnessed any more wonderful scene than the vast halls and courts of the El Azhar Mosque, thickly thronged with thousands of students, diligently committing to memory the sacred book of Islam, or listening with rapt attention to the lectures of venerable sheikhs expounding the commentaries on the Koran, and with eager faces propounding questions to their teachers. Here, if anywhere, we might expect to find a "hotbed of Mahommedan fanaticism." But what was the fact? An opportunity was afforded me of conversing with a group of some twenty of the students of El Azhar, and the result of this conversation, and of some statements in the vernacular newspapers that I was endeavouring to promote a friendly feeling between Christians and Mahommedans, was that I thought it prudent to avoid a proximate visit to El Azhar; having been warned that an inconvenient "ovation" was being prepared for me by the students when next I visited the mosque. I fearlessly assert that any one who goes among them as a well-wisher and a friend, without offensive assumptions of superior enlightenment, but endeavouring honestly to understand them, and dwelling on points of agreement as well as on points of difference, will be warmly welcomed and received.

It is, I think, the hostile polemic tone adopted by missionaries which is chiefly to blame for the conspicuous want of success which attends their efforts. Of this I had a curious illustration. I had a long and friendly discussion with a learned Mahommedan, which turned chiefly on the doctrine of the Trinity, which I found he wholly misapprehended, believing that Christians were practically Tritheists. This I told him was not the case ; and I explained the technical theological meaning of the word "person" in the Athanasian Creed, and expounded the Hegelian doctrine of the three possible and necessary modes in which the human mind can have cognizance of the Divine existence. This, I found, presented no difficulty to him, as it is nearly identical with the doctrines of the Bab, one of the Mahommedan sects. Shortly afterwards the ladies of our party visited the harem of this gentleman, when the result of the discussion was apparent from the apprehensions expressed by his wife that her husband was about to become a Christian. His chief objection to Christianity had plainly been based on a radical misconception of Christian belief.

Such misconceptions might be dispelled if men of the right sort were sent out to explain the doctrines of Christianity, or if men like my correspondent, the Turkish Bey, were brought to England to be initiated into the real nature of Christian teaching. I do not suppose that the future creed of Eastern lands will be either the narrow Puritanism of the Westminster Confession, against which even Scotch Presbyterians are beginning to rebel ; or the Elizabethan compromise set forth in the Anglican Articles and Prayer-book ; far less will it be the Mariolatry which is already losing its hold over Southern Europe ; but there are many Mahommedans who would not repudiate some form of Christianity approaching either the Socinianism into which so many of the English Presbyterians have lapsed, the Arianism of Ulphilas and the Goths, the semi-Arianism of Milton, or the Sabellianism of Paul of Samosata, of Emanuel Swedenborg, or of Dr. Isaac Watts. Indeed, there are not a few Mahommedans whose tenets are already practically Sabellian or Swedenborgian. Some however incline rather to Unitarianism. The *Inquirer* of the 31st of March, 1888, reports a conversation with an Indian Moslem, Mahommed Auzum Saheb, who stated that the "advanced Christian Theism" of the English Unitarians "would find a hearty acceptance among a large class of educated Mahommedans." The reporter of this conversation, a Unitarian minister who has been travelling in India, states as the result of his inquiries that those Mahommedans who belong to the reforming party "reject nearly all that we should reject, and accept most of what we should accept." We do not usually deny the Christian name to the English Unitarians, who hold the chapels and are the lineal successors of the two thousand Presbyterian clergymen who were ejected from the pulpits of the Church by the Act of Uniformity; nor will it be forgotten that a Unitarian minister was a member of the Company for the Revision of the Bible, and was allowed to receive the Holy Communion in Westminster Abbey. Possibly the time may come when Mahommedans, who do not differ greatly from English Unitarians in their interpretation of the New Testament, may be designated, if they desire it, by the name of Unitarian Christians.

In some respects the Mahommedans go further than many of the Unitarians in their recognition of the divine character of Jesus Christ. They accept fully the doctrine of His miraculous conception, they call Him the Messiah, and they never mention Him without profound reverence, always adding the words, "Blessed be His Name." They find no difficulty in St. John's doctrine of the Logos. One of my friends, after stating that the Messiah might be rightly termed the Incarnate Word of God, goes on to say, we " may confidently affirm that ' in the beginning was the Word, and the Word was with God, and the Word was God.' The Will precedes the Word ; but as we cannot form any correct conception of time before creation, for the two began together, it would not be quite correct to say that the Will went before the Word." This is not so very far from the doctrine of the Athanasian Creed.

It is often said that Mahommedans deny that Jesus Christ was the Son of God. This is not altogether true. They accept the statement of the Nicene Creed, that He was " conceived by the Holy Ghost ; " but they would reject with horror any words which might seem to imply an amour between the Supreme Being and a mortal maiden, such as those of which we read in Greek mytho- logy, and they would consider as blasphemous the statement of a Roman Cardinal *est etiam matrimonium inter Deum et B.V.M.* What they object to is the use of the Arabic word *walad*, " son," which etymologically implies physical pro- creation ; but they are willing to admit that the Messiah may be rightfully called *Ibnu 'llah*, which also means " Son of God," the word *ibn*

coming from another root which simply signifies
" birth."

Their belief as to the Crucifixion is the most
serious, perhaps the only insuperable obstacle in
the way of their acceptance of the Christian creeds.
It is the more difficult to meet, inasmuch as it is
not, like the foregoing, a mere philological misconception, but is based entirely on moral grounds.
The Mahommedans consider that it would be
unworthy of an Almighty Being, merciful and
compassionate, to have permitted One who did
no sin to be cruelly put to death. They
prefer to believe that, as in the case of Isaac,
a type of Christ, a substitute was provided by
Almighty power, most of them adopting some
form of Gnostic heresy, either the Valentinian,
the Marcionite, or the Basilidan. Some of them
think a *simulacrum* was miraculously created and
crucified ; others are of opinion that it was either
Judas Iscariot or Simon of Cyrene who was put
to death.

I have set forth as fully and candidly as I am
able the points of agreement and difference between
Mahommedans and ourselves ; but what has most
surprised me was their readiness to discuss their
beliefs, and their evident desire to bring their
doctrines into harmony with ours, so as to reconcile

the teaching of their two sacred books, the Koran and the Bible.

There can be no doubt that thoughtful Mahommedans are themselves coming to the conclusion that great changes are imminent, in doctrine as well as in practice. "The progress of thought," writes one of them, "is chiefly evidenced by the views which the great majority of Moslems now entertain respecting the institutions of polygamy, slavery, and the facility of divorce. Whatever may have been the necessity of polygamy in the earliest stages of society, in modern times it can only be regarded as an unmitigated and unendurable evil." This is owing, he continues, "to a better appreciation of the spirit of the Koran."

That in any measurable time we shall succeed in converting the Mahommedans to Christianity, I see no reason to expect; but that Islam may ultimately be transformed into a religion approximating much more closely than it now does to Christianity does not seem impossible. In some respects we are ourselves adopting Islamic teaching. Total abstinence, for example, is becoming an article of the creed of many earnest Christians. And Mahommedans point out that Luther's Reformation, so far as it was directed against image-worship, Mariolatry, celibacy, and sacerdotal pretensions, was a movement directed to the same objects as the earlier reformation of Mahommed. It cannot be denied, they say, that Protestantism differs less from Islam than Romanism does, while those Protestant sects which have gone furthest from Rome have approached nearer to Islam than the rest.

# XVI.

## FROM A LADY'S DIARY.

THE attractions which Egypt offers to winter exiles in the way of climate, scenery, and objects of interest, is making it year by year a more formidable rival to Rome and the Riviera. I am told that during the last season more than five thousand arrivals were registered at Messrs. Cook's offices in Cairo. As intending visitors may wish to know something of the sort of life they may expect to lead, I transcribe for their benefit a few extracts from the diary and letters of one of the ladies of our party :—

"*Luxor, December* 24*th*, 1887.—We arrived here by rail and steamboat in about three days from Cairo. The hot, dusty railway journey to Assiout was unpleasant, but the voyage made up for it. Nothing could be more delightful than gliding peacefully on the broad river, sitting under the deck-awning, and watching the constantly changing and ever beautiful hills, which at times approach the Nile in precipitous cliffs, and then suddenly trend away into the far distance. The sunsets were magnificent, and the effect of the after-glow is hardly exaggerated in Holman Hunt's picture. We were fortunate in having the boat nearly to ourselves, and our fellow-travellers were intelligent and agreeable. We landed about midday, and stepped across the prostrate statue of an Egyptian king into an avenue of scented cassis trees in full flower, forming a shady tunnel up to the hotel, which stands in a charming grove of palm-trees.

" The landing-place is a dismantled steamboat moored alongside a broad, sandy quay, which stretches for a quarter of a mile between the Nile and the great Luxor temple, forming a sort of promenade. Close to the entrance of the hotel are the massive walls of the inner shrine, built of huge stones covered with sculptures and inscriptions. Part of the outer wall is broken down, owing, it is said, to the temple having been converted into a fortress when Thebes was besieged by one of the Ptolemies. Beyond the sanctuary, which still retains its roof of enormous slabs, is a large open court, surrounded on three sides by a double row of columns, imitating bundles of lotus plants tied together.

A little further we come to a colonnade of still more gigantic pillars with bell-shaped capitals, forming the approach to a smaller temple, containing colossal statues of Rameses II., which are partly hidden by a mosque and some mud houses, built against the walls. Beyond this temple are two huge sloping masses of masonry, covered with battle scenes, which constitute the great pylon or gateway, outside of which stands a solitary granite obelisk, whose fellow now adorns the Place de la Concorde at Paris.

"*December 27th.*—I really think Luxor is the most charming place I ever was in. After breakfast I take a book, and climb up to a favourite perch among the huge stones of the temple, and sit there gazing at the glorious Theban hills across the river, or trying to learn the grand old ruin by heart. The climate is quite perfect. The brilliant sunshine and the pure, delicious air from the desert make one feel in a delightful happy-go-lucky frame of mind. Worries and bothers do not take hold of one as they do in England; the mere animal delight of being alive is sufficient for complete happiness. No one is in a hurry; there is nothing to do, and plenty of time to do it in. It is not even necessary to know what o'clock it is, as there are no clocks,

and no two watches are alike ; while as the post
to England goes only once a week, and as there
are no trains to catch, and no appointments to
keep—even dinner being a movable feast—time
ceases to be of consequence.

"On the quay itself there is always a good
deal of picturesque native life going on. A camel-
load of sugar-cane is brought every morning for
sale, and thrown down in front of the temple,
and a group of Arabs is everlastingly squatting
round it, chewing contentedly, whilst a camel,
buffalo, or donkey is made happy with the green
tops. The buffaloes are unprepossessing looking
animals, mangy and nearly hairless. There is
one especially who haunts the temple, and
nothing comes amiss to her in the way of food.
The other day she came sniffing round me, and
made an attempt to eat my 'Murray,' as a welcome change from the stones and sand which are
the only pasture the temple affords. No wonder
that the butter and milk are of inferior quality !
Now and then a boat-load of native pottery is
landed on the quay, and the owner sits on the
ground for a day or two, barricaded by his goods,
till they gradually melt away, after some hard
bargaining. Then a tourist walks by, and is
pertinaciously assailed by vendors of *antikas*, such

as blue beads, alabaster vases, figures of Egyptian deities, Ptolemaic coins, *ushabtis*, mummy cloth, and all sorts of spoils obtained from the tombs. I have just been watching, with great amusement, a strong-minded lady, resolutely carrying an enormous sketching apparatus, and struggling with an officious crowd of small boys, who vainly endeavoured to relieve her of her burden.

"*December* 30*th.*—Yesterday I saw four persons returning from a camel-ride, with looks of suppressed agony on their countenances. It was funny to remark the expression of relief which came over their faces when the camels knelt down to allow them to dismount. They were evidently thankful they had safely accomplished, once for all, one of the necessary experiences of an Egyptian tour. I have already had an expedition on a camel, and do not care to repeat it, though it was very pleasant to ride round Karnak, and see the vast enclosure from such a height. The camel is a cross-tempered beast to ride, but the Egyptian donkey is a charming creature. No experience of the English animal gives any idea of them ; they are large, spirited, and handsome, with very pleasant paces. Occasionally you may get a bad one, but, as a rule, they are excellent. The largest of the Luxor donkeys, appropriately called

Rameses, carries easily a gentleman who is reputed to weigh sixteen stone. Everybody in their turn expects a tumble; but the distance from the ground is not great, and the sand is soft. At Dendera my donkey came down on his nose, sending me softly and completely over his head; but I was up and on again directly, not a bit the worse.

"The costumes of the natives are delightful and of endless variety; I have not seen two men dressed alike. Some are in snowy white night-gowns with a girdle, others in gorgeously coloured silk petticoats, with jackets of some other hue. Every shade of blue is worn, and 'Liberty' colours abound. The turbans are especially fascinating. As a rule, the Arabs are sufficiently clothed, though occasionally you see men making bricks, or working their shadoofs, with very little more covering than the garb bestowed on them by nature. But even then, the lovely rich Vandyke-brown colour of the skin, and their perfect dignity and simplicity, make them look quite respectable and proper. There is not nearly so much to be shocked at as in many an English ball-room. One elderly young lady expressed her disgust at the sight of some dusky little naked cherubs who were capering round her donkey,

L

and "wondered that their mammas were not ashamed to let them go out in such a state;" but, for my part, I own I feel more inclined to share Lady Duff Gordon's admiration for the little brown babies she used to be so fond of.

"*January 2nd.*—There are four villages which occupy portions of the site of Thebes. Luxor and Karnak are on this, the eastern side of the Nile, and on the other, or western side, lie the ruins at the Ramesseum, Medinet Habou, and Gourneh, with the desolate valley beyond leading up to the tombs of the kings. All formed part of an enormous city. It is much as if London were destroyed, and the site occupied by green fields intersected by the Thames, with the ruins of a few great buildings, such as the Tower, St. Paul's, Westminster Abbey, the British Museum, and the Marble Arch, standing at distant intervals.

"Karnak is nearly two miles from Luxor. They were formerly connected by an avenue of sphinxes, which have now almost entirely disappeared. One of our earliest visits to Karnak was by moonlight— and such a moon as we never see in England. Those awful columns and gigantic pylons were weird and impressive beyond description; but the more ruinous portions, 'the wilderness of tumbled

walls, and the huge masses of riven masonry,'
are better seen by daylight. We have ridden to
Karnak many times, but it really seems impossible
ever to obtain a grasp of the whole group of mighty
buildings. So many ages were employed in their
construction, and the devastation has been so
great, that it is difficult to realize what it all
looked like at any given period of its history.
Now it is a stupendous pile of ruins—vaster and
far more impressive than the pyramids. The only
discordant elements in the calm of centuries that
broods over deserted Thebes are the occasional
parties of Cook's tourists, skurrying post-haste
through the temples, driven by an inexorable and
generally ignorant dragoman, who wants to get
the thing done in the shortest possible time, and
rattles off unreliable fragments of information in
broken English. Some of the tourists behave
disgracefully, and chip off, as relics, bits of carving
or painted hieroglyphs. A young foreign noble-
man amused himself by smearing the beautiful
paintings in the tomb of Seti I. with his tallow
candle, and could not be made to understand
that he was a barbarian of a bad type. Fortunately, most of the 'young barbarians' do not
care for antiquities. Speaking of the pyramids,
one of them observed, 'Beastly place ; been there

once, never want to go again!' And at Cairo most of them prefer the lawn-tennis ground at Shepheard's to the mosques or the bazaars.

"*January 3rd.*—The excursion to the western side of the Nile is rather a serious affair. We usually start soon after seven, before the heat begins, and when the fresh morning air is delicious. There are two branches of the river to be crossed ; the first, which is the main stream, is at this time of year too shallow, near the further bank, to admit of the boat getting close up to the shore, so one has to trust one's self to a couple of Arabs, to be carried in their arms through the water, clinging convulsively to their necks. It is an agonizing experience, but supremely comical when other people are the victims. The gentlemen have only one Arab apiece, and sit pick-a-back.

"When we are landed on the wet sandbank, we have to fight our way among a crowd of donkey-boys, all clamouring to be engaged. On one occasion our party was landed on a quicksand, and a stout gentleman, being hustled prematurely on to a donkey by a vociferous Arab, suddenly found his steed and himself disappearing in the quagmire. The unfortunate donkey was soon up to his girths, and was only got out after a great expenditure of blows and tugs from the excited crowd.

"A quarter of an hour's hot ride across the sandy island brings you to the second branch of the Nile, which has to be crossed in a rickety punt. The donkeys jump in first and take the best places, and the passengers huddle together on a little platform at the stern. On one occasion the punting-pole stuck in the mud, and, in endeavouring to pull it out, the Arab went head over heels into the water and disappeared. However, he soon came to the surface, gave his one garment a squeeze, and in a very short time it was completely dried by the sun.

"Once safely across the second stream, we remount our donkeys, and ride through the fresh green fields till we come to the famous statues of Memnon, and then pursue our way to one of the temples, or across the arid desert to the tombs, the midday sun pouring down upon us, and becoming hotter and hotter every moment.

"*January 5th.*—An absurd thing happened yesterday. It appears that Mr. Cook had an idea of setting up a weekly *Luxor Gazette*, with the resident doctor as author, editor, printer, and publisher. A printing press was sent out from England, with a plentiful supply of type. When the doctor came to dinner, we noticed a mingled expression of fury and despair on his countenance; and, on questioning him, it turned out that the separate parcels of type had been packed in brown paper, which had got damp on the voyage and had burst, the result being unutterable confusion. There was about a couple of bushels of what printers call ' pie,' and the unfortunate doctor had been engaged for five hours trying to sort it, and, as he ruefully remarked, he did not seem to have made the smallest impression on the pile. The publication of the *Luxor Gazette* has consequently been indefinitely postponed.

" *January* 16*th.*—I am working hard at Arabic, and have a lesson every day from the telegraph clerk, whose knowledge of English is limited and peculiar. At first all the letters look alike; but, when once that difficulty is mastered, it is easier to get on. The pronunciation of the gutturals is quite dreadful, and my teacher tells me that there are thirty-five different ways of forming the plural ; but the words are so expressive that they are not difficult to remember. I find I can already manage some short sentences, and the donkey-boys are always eager to give instruction, so that every ride becomes a lesson.

"Most of the visitors have learnt a few Arabic words, which are almost necessary in the outlying villages ; the most useful being, *Emshi ruh,* 'Go away ;' *Mush auz,* 'I don't want it ;' *Kettir khay-rak,* 'Much obliged ;' *taib,* good ; *mush taib,* bad ; *la,* no ; *Neharak saida,* 'Good morning ;' *Liltak saida,* 'Good night ;' and a few *mashal-lahs, bismillahs,* and *inshallahs* can be thrown in at discretion. The Arabic numerals, up to ten, are very handy in making purchases. *Bukra fil mishmish* is an invaluable joke with which to get rid of an importunate crowd. It means, I believe, that you will distribute 'green apricots to-morrow,' and is received with unfailing delight.

" Almost all the donkey-boys have learnt a little English, which they are very fond of airing. Some of their phrases are very amusing. Thus a beggar boy represents that he is an orphan, and in need of alms—'Father finish ! mother finish ! poor man ! backsheesh !' A lad thus described to us the uses of a tug that lay at anchor off Ismailia— 'Big ship go stick, him go catch.' Your attendant of the previous day lies in wait for you at the door of the hotel, and accosts you with, 'Me Achmet, me friend for you,' or 'Me Mahomet, me ready for you.' When your bargaining is concluded, you say, 'Finish buy,' and the dealers go off to bother some one else.

"*January 29th.*—We sat up last night till two o'clock to see the eclipse of the moon, and it was well worth our while. The appearance of the stars was most wonderful. They were hardly visible before the eclipse began, owing to the brilliant light of the moon. ' It was *so* fortunate,' as a lady remarked to me, 'that we happened to have a full moon for the eclipse.' The moon darkened till nothing was left of her but a bronze disc, with a ruddy glow in the centre ; then the stars streamed out in dazzling beauty, and as the light of the moon reappeared, they gradually faded away again. The whole population of Luxor perambulated the village for two hours, chanting prayers and beating toms-toms. The next day we got the following explanation from one of the natives : ' Moon go wrong ; want Lord to make moon go straight. If moon go wrong, we not know when sow corn, when say prayers.' We afterwards got the exact words of the Arabic chant, which a Copt translated as follows : ' O my Lord, look and see; some of us are children, the others are men; we are Thy servants, O Lord ; the order is in Thy hand.' We afterwards found that this ceremony prevails in other Mahommedan countries. When Mahomed's son died there was an eclipse, and the people thought the moon was mourning for the child's death ; but Mahomed reproved them, saying, 'The sun and the moon are signs appointed by Allah ; but they are not eclipsed because of the death of any mortal. When ye observe an eclipse, betake yourselves to prayer until it passeth away.'

"*February* 1st.—The Southern Cross has lately been an object of keen interest in the hotel. One of the regular winter residents affirmed that it was not visible in this latitude ; but, fortunately, we had a good star map, which proved the contrary to be true. We calculated that it would rise about three o'clock in the morning. So we roused ourselves from sleep, and had the satisfaction of seeing it blazing away due south, with the lowest star almost touching the horizon. Next night half the hotel got up in the small hours to see it, and those who had rooms with a southern aspect held 'at homes' to meet the Southern Cross.

"*February* 8th.—Alas! we have left Luxor ; but, as a consolation, we have been to the first cataract and Philæ. The trip took us five days, and we managed to see a good deal in the time. Each day the boat stopped for us to visit some temple, and at Assouan we had a day and a half, and went through the bazaars, and got some of the Nubian pottery. Philæ is a rocky island with lovely Ptolemaic temples. We went from Assouan by railway six miles across the desert. It grew very hot towards midday, and we were almost baked as we walked down in the afternoon to the cataract, which is a series of foaming rapids interspersed with black granite islets. Twenty or thirty black savages, nearly naked, sprang into the water, and shot the cataract on logs of wood, and then, scrambling out, rushed at us, howling for backsheesh, and almost laying violent hands upon us. One of our party had a kourbash, and laid about him freely, which cleared the ground a little, and we were glad to take refuge as soon as possible in the boat which was waiting for us, leaving the yelling mob on the shore. It was my first taste of real savagery, and I cannot say I liked it. We had a lovely ride back through the valley of rocks and across the desert, in the cool of the evening, and visited the half-quarried obelisk which has been lying unfinished for unknown centuries, with chips of granite, fresh, as it were, from the workman's chisel, lying all round.

" Coming down the river we had an experience of a dust storm or simoon. The day had been close and dull ; all at once we noticed a dark grey curtain advancing rapidly along the Nile. It came from the south-west, and in a moment, mountains, plain, river, sun, were all blotted out, and the air became full of the finest sand, while a fierce hot wind raged round us. The awning of the steam-boat was taken down, or it would have been torn to shreds. Everything was covered with dust, and we all took refuge in our cabins. Fortunately, it did not last long, and we were thankful to see the sun reappear.

"*Cairo, February 27th.*—We have had another delightful three weeks in Cairo. It has not lost its charm, and we are more loth to leave it than ever, though it is getting unpleasantly warm. Egypt spoils one for every other country, even for Italy. Cairo is really too fascinating, wonderful beyond anything that I had imagined. I feel as if, like Alice, I had got behind some enchanted looking-glass, and had been living in the land of dreams. Passing through the good-humoured and many coloured crowd which throngs the narrow streets, one involuntarily gives the people names out of the 'Arabian Nights.' Here are Abou Hassan and Aladdin ; there go Zobeide and Amina. A sudden turn brings one in front of an exquisitely graceful mosque, with a slender minaret towering into the blue ; and lo, on the steps the one-eyed Calendar is sure to be sitting on his heels, awaiting our approach. Day after day we have been revisiting our favourite mosques, their walls and floors inlaid with encaustic tiles or precious marbles, or ornamented with the most intricate geometrical patterns, or verses from the Koran with the letters intertwined in the most ingenious manner. And there are a thousand other things—the Copts and their ancient churches, and the tombs of the Khalifs, and the howling dervishes, and the lonely obelisk that marks the site of Heliopolis, and the Pyramids, and the Sphinx, and Boulaq, with its wonderful treasures, and the sunsets from the citadel, the sun setting in a flood of golden light just behind the pyramids.

"And now, for the last time, we have ridden through the never-ending wonder of the bazaars, making final purchases of fascinating Oriental wares, bargaining in our best Arabic with the turbaned merchants for gaily striped silks, red Morocco slippers, and brass cups and trays engraved with quaint interlaced patterns and verses from the Koran. But, alas! Cook has sent a copy of a telegram from Aden, informing us that our ship has cut the record, and is two days before its time, so that we must start to-morrow for Ismailia. 'Please, Mr. Cook, can you change our tickets for some later steamer?' 'No, ma'am, quite impossible ; every berth is engaged for the next six weeks.' And so, most reluctantly, we take our leave of this enchanted land, with the earnest hope that some day we may visit it again. My wonder is, why everybody who can manage it does not come to Egypt every winter."

THE END.

PRINTED BY WILLIAM CLOWES AND SONS, LIMITED, LONDON AND BECCLES.